"You locked yourself in?"

The surprise in Flynn's voice needled Sandie afresh.

"Yes, I did," she said tautly. "And I'll continue to keep my door locked."

"A very virtuous resolution," he said mockingly. "But there are three things you haven't considered."

Her fingers tightened around each other. "I'm sure you're going to tell me what they are."

"Firstly, as owner of Killane, I could have a master key to all the rooms. Secondly, if I wanted a woman, no old rusty lock would keep me out. And thirdly—" He paused.

"Well?" Sandie prompted icily.

"Thirdly," said Flynn, "I could stop this vehicle here and now and persuade you to change your mind. And we both know it."

SARA CRAVEN probably had the ideal upbringing for a budding writer. She grew up by the seaside in a house crammed with books, a box of old clothes to dress up in and a swing outside in a walled garden. She produced the opening of her first book at age five and is eternally grateful to her mother for having kept a straight face. Now she has more than twenty-five novels to her credit. The author is married and has two children.

Books by Sara Craven

Don't miss any of our special offers. Write to us at the following address for information on our newest releases.

Harlequin Reader Service
901 Fuhrmann Blvd., P.O. Box 1397, Buffalo, NY 14240
Canadian address: P.O. Box 603,
Fort Erie, Ont. L2A 5X3

SARA CRAVEN

island of the heart

Harlequin Books

TORONTO • NEW YORK • LONDON
AMSTERDAM • PARIS • SYDNEY • HAMBURG
STOCKHOLM • ATHENS • TOKYO • MILAN

For John and Evangeline Roche
and all the friends I found
at the Rock Glen, Clifden.

Harlequin Presents first edition February 1990
ISBN 0-373-11241-6

Original hardcover edition published in 1989
by Mills & Boon Limited

CHAPTER ONE

THE last chords sang their way triumphantly into the echoing silence, and Sandie Beaumont lifted her hands from the keyboard as the applause began.

The adrenalin which had carried her through the performance was already starting to subside as she rose and bowed to the clapping audience. She kept her hands hidden in the folds of her violet taffeta skirt to disguise the fact that they were shaking.

Listening intently, she tried to judge the audience reaction to her playing. It was enthusiastic, but was it the kind of acclaim accorded to a winner? Sandie wasn't sure.

She deliberately avoided even a glance towards the row of judges seated behind their table at the front of the auditorium. She would know their verdict soon enough.

'It's not the end of the world.' That was what one of her fellow contestants had said as he'd left the waiting-room backstage where they were all assembled an hour earlier.

And in a way it wasn't. It was a piano contest in a newly established music festival, that was all. A first rung on the ladder to such glories as the Leeds Piano Competition.

But for me, Sandie thought, as she bowed again, and made her way with forced composure off the platform, for me, it could easily be the end of everything.

There was a long mirror at the end of the corridor leading back to the dressing-rooms. She'd been too nervous to use it on her way to the platform, but she paused now to glance at herself, swiftly and clinically. Too pale, she thought. She should have used more blusher. In the dim light of the passage, with her silvery blonde hair hanging straight and shining below her shoulders, she looked almost ghostly.

But the dress was wonderful. It had been an extravagance, but it was worth it, accentuating, as it did, the colour of her own violet eyes. It had made her feel good, given her the confidence to believe that everything was going to be all right. As if a career in music, as she'd always dreamed, was actually within reach.

Her hands balled into fists of tension, and she swallowed as she turned away. Well, she would soon know. She'd been the last competitor.

Back in the big room, where the others waited, no one was saying much. They were all on edge now, anticipating the call which would take them back on stage for the adjudication. Most of them seemed to know each other already—to be able to judge the standard they were up against. She, Sandie, was the outsider, the unknown quantity. The local girl taking her first step towards national fame—or instant obscurity.

Her parents had been quite adamant.

'My dear, you don't realise the kind of odds you're up against,' her father had said. 'Yes, you've got talent, I don't doubt, but that's not enough to make

you a star at international level. You may be Mrs
Darnley's prize pupil, but what does that really
mean?'

'I don't know,' Sandie had returned desperately.
'But you've got to let me find out.'

Her parents exchanged uneasy glances. She knew
what they were thinking. They were remembering
Sandie's grandmother, the Alexandra for whom she
had been named, whose considerable musical talent
had never taken her further than the orchestras of
second-rate touring variety shows and seaside concert
parties. For years she'd soldiered on, declaring her
big break would come—only it never had, and the
realisation that it never would had led to increasing
bouts of depression until her death, still in early
middle age.

They don't want that to happen to me, Sandie
thought. They don't want me to break my heart,
searching for some big time which may never come.

Aloud, she said, 'You've got to let me have my
chance.'

'Then we will.' Her father knocked out his pipe in
the ashtray. 'Mrs Darnley's entered you for the festival. If you can win it, you shall have your chance—
music college and the rest—whatever it takes. If you
don't win, then you give up all thoughts of a career
as a pianist. Is it agreed?'

'All or nothing—just like that?' Sandie stared at
them pleadingly. 'Mum, I . . .'

'Your father and I are in total agreement.' Mrs
Beaumont spoke more gently than her husband. 'It's
for your own sake, darling. After all, Sandie, you're

nineteen now. Most professional musicians started training years before you did.'

'That's hardly my fault.' Sandie remembered the uphill struggle to persuade her parents to allow her to have piano lessons at all.

'No,' her mother agreed. 'But you can't blame us for being cautious. It's time you put all this nonsense behind you, and trained for something—settled down. If it has to be music, you could always teach. You don't have to go on being a legal secretary, if you really hate it so much.' She gave Sandie an anxious smile. 'And you can always play the piano for your own amusement.'

Sandie had winced.

Mrs Darnley had been sympathetic, but had refused to take up the cudgels on Sandie's behalf.

'Your parents are doing what they feel is right,' she said. 'I can't argue about their natural concern for you. And they could have a point.'

Sandie stared at her. 'But I thought you believed in me,' she said, biting her lip. 'Don't you think I can make it?'

Mrs Darnley sighed. 'Sandie, you're the best pupil I've ever had, but that's all I can say. You've outgrown me, my dear. From now on, you need specialist coaching that I'm not qualified to give you—master classes. It all costs money, and if your parents aren't prepared to make a contribution...' She left it at that.

Now, weeks later, Sandie looked under her lashes at her fellow competitors and wondered. They all wanted to win—that went without saying. But did any of them have the compulsive, driving need to come first that she possessed?

She thought, My whole future depends on this.

It seemed an eternity before the recall to the platform came. They filed on and stood trying to look nonchalant and modest at the same time. Sandie's legs were shaking, and her mouth felt dry. She wanted it over with. She wanted to *know*.

The judges moved on to the platform, and she studied them unobtrusively, trying to read their faces, to see if they looked longer in one direction than another.

The tall man standing at the end caught her eye and smiled, and she felt herself blush.

She knew who he was, of course. They were all musical celebrities, but he was the star. Crispin Sinclair, the youngest of the four, had been a young virtuoso pianist himself some years before, spoken of as a prodigy. He was one of Sandie's heroes, and she had several of his recordings. But in recent years, he'd turned from the concert platform to composition. He'd written a modern opera based on Sean O'Casey's *Juno and the Paycock*, which had been received with acclaim on both sides of the Atlantic, as well as a host of shorter works, many of them commissioned. One of them was to be performed at the end of the festival, and Crispin Sinclair himself was going to conduct.

It was also rumoured that, under different names, he'd written music for various well-known pop groups.

But he'd had a head start in the musical world, Sandie thought, staring embarrassedly at the floor. His mother was Magda Sinclair, the world-famous mezzo-soprano and opera star, and his sister Jessica was already a noted cellist.

No one in his family would have ever jibbed at his choice of occupation. He would have been encouraged and nursed along since babyhood, and the first signs of precocious talent.

Whereas I didn't even have a piano until I was thirteen, Sandie thought, with a sigh.

All the same, she couldn't help wondering if the smile he'd sent her held any significance.

She tried to concentrate on what the chairman of the judging panel was saying. There were the usual platitudes about the excellent organisation, and thanks to the patrons and sponsors before he turned to 'the wealth of talent here tonight,' 'the distinctive performances', 'the difficulty of reaching a decision, although the panel had been unanimous...'

Oh, get on with it, Sandie prayed silently, her insides knotting with tension.

'The results will be in reverse order,' he was saying, and paused in anticipation of the laugh. 'Just like Miss World.' He consulted the paper in his hand. 'In third place—Jennifer Greenslade.'

Applause broke out. Sandie watched the other girl, no more than fourteen, go up to get her prize, her face flushed with pleasure.

'And in second place——' the chairman paused theatrically, making the most of it, 'Alexandra Beaumont.'

More applause. Sandie heard it from a distance—from some limbo of pain and disappointment.

She had to force herself to move, terrified that her legs would betray her, and that she'd collapse there and then in front of them all. But of course she didn't. She took her prize envelope, shook hands, and managed to smile and say something polite as she was congratulated.

She didn't see or hear who came first. She went back to her place, alone, lost in a little nightmare world of despair and failure.

She couldn't look at the audience, at the place where she knew her parents were sitting. They'd be disappointed for her, she knew, but relieved as well. She'd done well, and justified Mrs Darnley's good opinion, but not quite well enough, so now the whole nonsensical idea could be abandoned, and life return to normal.

Normality, she thought bleakly. A teachers' training college, or a solicitors' office. That was the choice now.

She was thankful when the ceremony was over and she could escape to the privacy of the small dressing-room she'd been allocated. She pulled off that mockery of a taffeta dress, slinging it carelessly on to a chair in the corner before struggling back into the sweatshirt and jeans she'd worn earlier.

The tap on the door startled her. She tugged the sweatshirt down into place, scooping her long hair free of its collar. She supposed it would be her father and mother, knocking tactfully in case she was upset. But she was too aching, too stunned to cry. Tears would come later, she thought.

She called, 'Yes?' and the door opened, and Crispin Sinclair walked in.

'So this is the right room.' When he smiled, his teeth were very white. 'I came to offer my condolences. It was a very near thing, actually.'

'So near and yet so far,' Sandie said. She tried to speak lightly, but her voice broke a little in the middle.

'So I understand,' he said. 'I've been having an il-luminating chat with your teacher, and she told me it was make or break for you. That's really tough.'

He was one of the most attractive men Sandie had ever encountered, dark-haired and blue-eyed, and his smile was devastating. Suddenly the dressing room seemed tinier than ever.

She hastily picked up a comb and began to tug it through her hair. 'Well,' she said, 'you win some, you lose some.'

His brows lifted. 'Are you really that philosophical about it?'

'No,' she said baldly. 'But I've no other choice.'

'Maybe you have at that,' Crispin Sinclair said slowly. 'That old fool Gregory said we were unani-mous, but that was public relations. Actually, I was in there fighting for you. And now that I know how important that win would have been, I have a prop-osition for you.'

'For me?' She stared at him. 'I don't understand...'

He laughed. 'I haven't explained it yet.' He paused. 'But first, a little criticism. You performed the set pieces well, but your own choice was unadventurous, to say the least. That could have lost your first place.'

'It's a difficult movement...'

'Not when your basic technique's as good as yours. You should have taken a stance—gone for broke, like the guy who won did with the Prokofiev. You've been well taught, but now you need more.' He smiled at her equably. 'I think it's time I took you on myself.'

Sandie's eyes widened in incredulity. 'You—want to teach—me? But why?'

'I think it could be rewarding. I also think you deserve another chance, rather than having to rely on this sudden death situation you've been in. No one at your level can do her best with that kind of threat hanging over her.'

He scooped the taffeta dress off the chair and on to a hanger in an undoubtedly practised movement. 'Pity to spoil it, because it's a good platform dress—catches the light well, but doesn't take over.' He pushed the chair towards her. 'Sit down. You look as if you need to.'

Sandie subsided in limp obedience. She said in a little rush, 'I'm a junior secretary with a law firm. I don't know the kind of fees you charge, but I couldn't afford even half of them.'

'Well, there's a way round that.' Crispin Sinclair seated himself on the dressing stool. 'My family have taken themselves off for their usual summer break in Connemara, to rest and prepare for the next concert season, but my mother's regular practice accompanist has just got married, silly bitch, and to an oil man who's whisked her off to Venezuela. This has left Mama in quite a spot. She's inclined to be temperamental, but she liked Janet and she was used to her.' He paused. 'If you came to Killane, you could take Janet's place, and—work your passage, as it were.'

'But I don't know the first thing about accompanying anyone,' Sandie protested feverishly. 'It's a skilled profession.'

'You're talented and intelligent, and you wouldn't be appearing in public, after all. Magda would soon teach you the ropes.' He grinned. 'Blood on the keyboard and all that. Does the thought put you off?'

'No,' she denied instantly. Summer, she thought, in a house filled with music. She paused. 'Did you say—Connemara?'

'Yes. Magda's first husband was Irish, and he left her a life interest in the house. He was killed in a hunting accident while Flynn was still a baby. She's two husbands further on now, but she still spends her summers at Killane, although the damp can't be good for her throat. The house really belongs to Flynn, my half-brother, of course, but he's rarely there.'

'Flynn.' Sandie tried the name. 'Is he a musician too?'

'God, no!' Crispin's laugh was faintly derisive. 'Magda's always said he's some kind of changeling. He hasn't a note of music in his body, even though he spent his formative years touring with her. She'd put her career into cold storage when she married, but took it up again in a hurry when she found herself a penniless young widow. And the rest, as they say, is history.'

'So what does he do?'

'My father's family were merchant bankers, and they lured him into commerce.' Again Sandie sensed a faint sneer. 'Now he's a high-powered financial consultant, dealing mainly with tax advice for the rich and famous. He even keeps my mother on the straight and narrow. God only knows where he gets it from. Neither she nor his father had any head for figures at all,' he added with a shrug. 'But that's enough about Flynn. Are you prepared to give up your summer to a madhouse in the west of Ireland?'

Sandie said, with a catch in her voice, 'It sounds wonderful. But what will your mother say—having a stranger foisted on her?'

'You won't be a stranger. I'll explain the position, and you'll arrive with the backing of my warmest recommendation. How's that?'

'It can't be that simple.'

'Where are the complications?'

'Well, have you ever had a private pupil before? I mean—won't your family think it's odd, if I suddenly appear...?' She looked away, reddening slightly.

'I know what you mean, Miss Alexandra Beaumont.' Crispin sounded amused, then his voice sobered. 'I'm asking you to Killane because I think you have a worthwhile talent which you won't otherwise have the opportunity to exploit.' He paused, then said deliberately, 'Let's leave any other considerations in the lap of the gods, shall we? Now, do you accept my proposition?'

Sandie's heart was thumping swiftly and painfully against her ribs. She could feel other objections crowding in. She was assailed by nervousness and exhilaration at the same time.

She said, 'Yes, I do. But I don't know what my parents will say.'

'Leave them to me,' he said. 'I'll handle them.' He rose, and so did she. 'Now, shall we seal our bargain in the time-honoured way?'

He held out his hand, and Sandie put her fingers into his, only to find herself drawn forward to receive Crispin's light kiss on her mouth.

He said, 'I'll be in touch,' then the dressing room door closed behind him.

Sandie stared after him, her hand lifting involuntarily to touch her lips.

She thought, A summer in Connemara. It sounds like magic—too good to be true. She hesitated. But after the summer—what then?

She shrugged. I'll wait and see, she told herself, and let the remembrance of Crispin Sinclair's smile dispel that faint chill of anxiety inside her.

A fortnight later, still dazed at the total upheaval in her life, Sandie found herself descending from the plane at Shannon.

Looking back, she realised she had never thought her parents would agree, and she hadn't the slightest idea how Crispin had persuaded them. Neither, she thought, had they. But she was aware that he'd accentuated her dubious role as his mother's accompanist rather than her status as his pupil, and although this wasn't exactly a deception, it had caused her a slight flicker of uneasiness.

Inside the terminal building, she collected her luggage and made her way to the Aer Lingus desk as Crispin had instructed.

'Excuse me,' she addressed the green-clad girl, who looked up smiling at her approach. 'My name is Beaumont. Someone is meeting me here.'

The girl nodded. 'Your man was just enquiring for you,' she said. She looked past Sandie, and beckoned.

Sandie turned to find herself confronted by a short, squat individual. His face was as brown and wrinkled as a walnut, and his greying hair still held a tinge of fierce red. He was staring at Sandie with an expression of incredulity that was too disconcerting to be amusing.

'It's you, is it, I'm to take to Killane?' His tone held lively dismay.

Sandie tilted her chin a little. 'I'm Mr Sinclair's guest, yes,' she returned coolly. 'How do you do, Mr—er——?' She held out her hand.

'O'Flaherty will do—without the Mister.' The man ignored her hand, and picked up her cases. 'Guest,' he added with a faint snort. 'Well for Mr Crispin that himself's not at home to see this.' And on this obscure utterance, he turned and strode towards the main doors, heading for the car park. Sandie had to run in order to keep up with him.

She said breathlessly, and a little desperately, 'I am expected, aren't I?'

'They're expecting someone, surely.' Sandie's cases were fitted into the back of a large estate car. 'In you get, now. We have a fair drive ahead of us.'

Sandie got into the passenger seat and fastened its belt. It was not the introduction she'd expected to Ireland of the Hundred Thousand Welcomes, she thought, trying to feel amused, and failing.

'It's a beautiful day,' she tried tentatively, as they won free of the airport's environs, and embarked on the road to Galway.

'It won't last,' was the uncompromising reply, and Sandie sighed soundlessly, and transferred her attention to the scenery.

It took well over an hour to reach Galway. Beyond the city, the road narrowed dramatically, and the weather, as O'Flaherty had predicted, began to deteriorate. Ahead, Sandie could see mountains, their peaks hidden by cloud, and the whole landscape seemed to be changing, taking on a disturbing wildness now that the narrow grey towns had been left behind.

O'Flaherty had wasted no time with his driving so far, but now he slowed perceptibly, as the rattle of loose chippings stung at the underside of the car. Moorland rolled away on both sides of the road, interspersed with a scatter of small white houses, most of them with thatched roofs. Here and there, the earth had been deeply scarred by turf cutting, and piles of turfs stood stacked and awaiting collection near the verges. There were great stretches of water too, looking grey and desolate under the lowering sky. Some of the lakes had islands, and Sandie, fascinated, spotted the ruined stones of an ancient tower on one, half hidden by trees and undergrowth. She would have loved to have asked its history, but after sneaking a look at O'Flaherty's forbidding countenance she decided to save her questions for Crispin.

She was frankly puzzled by the little man's hostility, and it made her apprehensive about her reception generally when eventually they reached their journey's end. If they ever did, she thought, stretching her cramped legs in front of her.

'Too long a ride for you, is it?'

'No, I'm enjoying it,' Sandie said mendaciously. 'The scenery's fabulous, isn't it? So romantic.'

Her innocent comment was greeted by another snort, and silence descended again.

There was little other traffic—some cyclists, a lorry piled high with bales of hay, a few cars and a couple of horseboxes. Occasionally they were brought to a halt by sheep and cattle wandering across the road in front of them.

Rain splattered across the windscreen, and O'Flaherty swore under his breath, and flicked on the wipers, before turning off on to a side road bordering yet another enormous lake. The clouds were down so low now that only the lower slopes of the mountains were visible.

'What are they called?' Sandie asked, pointing.

'The Twelve Pins.'

The road unwound in front of them, like a narrow grey ribbon, edging the water. Sandie watched the rain dancing across the flat surface of the lake, and shivered a little, not from cold, but a sudden swift loneliness.

If she was at home now, she thought, she would probably be helping her mother in the garden, with its neat lawns and beds and well-pruned trees. And instead, here she was driving through a wilderness of water and peat bogs, to what?

She hadn't expected Crispin to be at the airport to meet her, but she wished with all her heart that he had been. Perhaps she wouldn't have been feeling quite so strange—and desolate, she thought swallowing a lump in her throat, as she realised just how far she was from home and everything familiar.

'There's Killane,' said O'Flaherty abruptly, and gestured towards where a broad promontory jutted out into the lake. Peering forward, Sandie could see a thin trail of smoke rising above the clustering trees and, as they got closer, could make out the outline of a house. He turned a car across a cattle grid, through empty gateposts, and up a long drive flanked on each side by tall hedges of fuchsia, growing wild in a profusion of pink, crimson and purple.

And then the house was there in front of them, big and square, like a child might draw, with long multi-paned windows. Stone steps, guarded by urns filled with trailing plants, led up to the double doors of the main entrance. It looked grand, forbidding and slightly shabby, all at the same time, Sandie decided wonderingly.

O'Flaherty brought the car to a halt at the foot of the steps. 'Away in with you,' he directed. 'I'll see to your luggage.'

Sandie flew through the raindrops up the steps, and turned the handle on one of the doors. It gave more easily than she anticipated, and she nearly fell into a wide hall, with a flagged stone floor.

'God bless us and save us!' exclaimed a startled voice.

As Sandie recovered her equilibrium, she found she was being observed by a tall grey-haired woman in a flowered overall, carrying a tray laden down with tea-things.

She said, 'I was told to come straight in. I am expected . . .'

It was beginning, she realised with exasperation, to sound a little forlorn. It was also irksome to find the woman gaping at her, rather as O'Flaherty had done at the airport.

Sandie straightened her shoulders. 'I'd like to see Mr Sinclair, please,' she said with a trace of crispness.

'He's in Galway, and won't be back till night. I'll take you to the madam.' The woman continued across the hall, to another pair of double doors, and

shouldered her way through them, indicating that
Sandie should follow.

It was a big room, filled comfortably with sofas
and chairs in faded chintz. A turf fire blazed on the
hearth, and a woman was sitting beside it. She was
dark-haired, with a vivid, striking face, lavishly made
up, and was wearing a smart dress in hyacinth blue
silk, with a wool tartan scarf wrapped incongruously
round her neck. Sandie recognised her instantly and
nervously.

'Here's the young lady come to play the piano for
Mr Crispin,' the woman who'd shown Sandie in announced, setting the tray down on an occasional table.

Sandie found herself being scrutinised from several
directions—by the woman beside the fire, by a tall,
dark girl, bearing a strong resemblance to Crispin,
and also by two children, a boy and girl barely in their
teens, bent over a jigsaw puzzle at another table.

'Oh, dear,' Magda Sinclair said at last. 'Oh, dear.
This is too bad of Crispin. This really won't do at
all.'

Sandie knew an ignominious and overwhelming
urge to burst into weary tears. She'd set out with such
high hopes, and come all this way, and now Crispin
wasn't here, and his mother disliked her on sight. She
remembered Crispin had said she was temperamental.

'Now, now, Mother.' The dark girl got up from the
window seat where she'd been sprawling, and came
forward. 'The poor kid will think she's landed in a
lunatic asylum!' She held out her hand. 'Hello, I'm
Jessica Sinclair. Welcome to Killane. This, as you
probably realise, is Magda Sinclair, and the brats are
James and Steffie.'

Sandie swallowed. 'How do you do. I'm Alexandra Beaumont.' She was beginning to feel like something in a zoo.

Magda Sinclair seemed to shake herself, and got up. 'I'm sorry, my dear, if we seem a little odd, but we just didn't expect you to look so—so...'

'Young,' her daughter supplied, with a hint of dryness, giving Sandie the impression this was not what Magda Sinclair had intended to say at all.

'Yes, of course,' Mrs Sinclair said. She gave Sandie a brief smile. 'I expect you've had a terrible journey. Why don't you let Bridie show you your room, then come down and have some tea with us.'

Sandie had been expecting to be shown the door, rather than the place where she was to sleep.

She said, 'Thank you. That would be marvellous.'

Bridie led the way back into the hall. As Sandie followed, the strap of her bag caught on the ornately carved doorknob, and she paused to disentangle it.

Through the half-open door, she heard Jessica Sinclair say in a low voice, 'Don't look so worried, Mother. Everything will be fine.' She paused, adding flatly, 'Just as long as Flynn stays a thousand miles away.'

CHAPTER TWO

SANDIE'S room was at the back of the house. Vast and high-ceilinged, it contained a cavernous wardrobe in walnut with elegant brass handles, and a matching dressing-table, tallboy and old-fashioned bedstead of equally generous proportions. Sandie felt almost dwarfed as she unpacked and put her things away.

Tea had been an awkward meal. Having behaved so strangely when she arrived, the Sinclairs now seemed embarrassingly over-eager to put her at her ease, Sandie found ruefully. In spite of that, she'd managed to drink two cups of the strong, fragrant tea, and sample some of Bridie's featherlight scones, and rich, treacly fruit loaf.

Bridie, she'd learned, was the cook-housekeeper, and the mainstay of the household.

'She came here as a kitchenmaid when I married Rory Killane,' Magda Sinclair explained, 'and she's been here ever since. She knows more about this family than we do ourselves, and she's incredibly loyal.'

'She likes Flynn best,' said James, passing his cup to be refilled.

'What nonsense,' his mother said coldly. 'She adores us all. Anyway, Flynn is never here.'

'Bridie says he'll be here soon. She saw it in the tea-leaves,' put in Steffie, heaping jam on to her fruit loaf.

25

Sandie saw Magda's exquisitely reddened lips form something that might have been 'Damnation' and hastily looked elsewhere. She hadn't intended to overhear that brief snatch of conversation before she went upstairs, but she couldn't help being intrigued by its implications.

Flynn Killane, she thought. Crispin's non-musical half-brother, who, for some mysterious reason, needed to be kept at a distance.

But what difference can it possibly make to him if I'm here or not? she asked herself in bewilderment.

As soon as she could, she'd excused herself from the tea-party round the drawing-room fire, on the grounds that she needed to unpack. But with that task accomplished, she needed to find something else to do until Crispin came back from Galway, and she was reluctant to return to the drawing-room with its spurious bonhomie, interspersed with silences.

She wandered over to the window and stood looking out. It was raining harder than ever, she noticed with a sigh, and the wind had risen, bending the trees and shrubs that fringed the lawn. Beyond the formal part of the garden was a white-painted fence, dividing it from a paddock where several horses grazed.

'Have you got everything you need?'

She swung round to see Jessica standing in the doorway, her smile friendly.

'Yes, thanks. This is a charming room.'

'I think it's totally bizarre, like all of them.' Jessica cast a droll glance towards the embroidered runners that masked the polished surfaces of the chests and bedside table, and the pin tray and trinket jars in rose-painted china which ornamented the dressing-table.

'It's like being caught in a Thirties timewarp. Fortunately, the plumbing is bang up to date. Flynn saw to that, although all our water comes from the lake.'

'It does?' Sandie's eyes widened, and Jessica grinned.

'Sounds rather primitive, eh? But it's the norm round here. It would cost a fortune to bring mains water to this scatter of population. We have a rain tank as well,' she added, nodding towards the streaming window. 'As you can see, it's rarely empty.' Her tone became brisker. 'Mother wondered whether you'd like to see the music-room, where you're going to be working.'

'Yes, I would—very much.' Sandie forced a smile. 'I began to wonder if I'd be staying, or whether I'd be asked to leave. Everyone keeps—staring at me as if they'd seen a ghost.'

'How rude of us,' Jessica said lightly. 'The fact is, you're the image of someone we used to know. The resemblance is quite amazing.'

So that's all, Sandie thought with relief. She said, 'Well, they say everyone has a double.'

'So they do.' Jessica's tone was faintly ironic. 'Come on, and I'll introduce you to the piano.'

The music-room was on the ground floor, at the side of the house.

'It used to be the morning-room,' Jessica explained as she led the way in, 'but Flynn had it converted to make the most of the view.'

Sandie gasped with pleasure. The entire end of the room had been extended out over the lake, and the walls and ceiling glazed so that sky and water formed

the backdrop for the magnificent Steinway grand that
stood there.

'It's fantastic!' she exclaimed.

'I'm glad you approve. You're going to be spending
a lot of your time here.' Jessica paused. 'Crispin can
be a hard taskmaster, but I suppose you know that.'

'I don't really know very much about him at all,'
Sandie returned. 'But he thinks I have promise as a
pianist, and I want to work hard for him.' She
swallowed. 'I hope Mrs Sinclair will let me try and
play her accompaniments. I need to justify my existence here.'

'I should find your feet before you start looking
for extra jobs,' Jessica said quite kindly. 'This room
is completely soundproofed, by the way, so you can
come and practise any time when no one else is using
it. I tend to work in my room, so you'll only have
Mother and Crispin to compete with.' She gestured
towards the piano. 'Go on, try it. I can see you're
dying to.' She disappeared, closing the door behind
her.

Sandie sat down and ran her fingers experimentally
over the keys. She began mutedly with scales, and a
few loosening exercises, then broke into the last
movement of the concerto she'd played at the festival.

When she finished, there was a burst of applause
from behind her, and she glanced round startled to
see Crispin standing in the doorway, smiling at her.

'Don't get up,' he directed, walking towards her.
'You look just as I imagined you would. This room
is the perfect background for you.'

Sandie flushed. 'I didn't come here to be orna-
mental,' she protested, with an awkward laugh.

'Of course not,' he said soothingly. 'But you can't escape the fact, sweetheart, that you are—amazingly decorative. I'm surprised your parents allowed you out of their sight.'

Her blush deepened, and she searched frantically for some casual and sophisticated response. I'm not very good at flirting, she thought despairingly. I've been so immersed in my music that there hasn't been time for men—or even boys. Of course, I know he isn't seriously interested in me in *that* way—he's just being—nice to me.

As he reached her, she wondered if he would kiss her again, and found herself both thrilled and a little nervous at the idea, but Crispin walked past to her to one of the long line of cupboards and extracted a pile of manuscript paper which he brought over to the piano.

'Here's something you might look at, when you have a moment,' he said. 'I call it *Elegy*.'

'You wrote this?' Sandie began to turn over the sheets.

'A long time ago. It's never had a public performance yet. I'm waiting for the right moment—and the right person to play it.' He smiled at her. 'Maybe that person will be you, Miss Alexandra Beaumont.'

'I shouldn't think so,' she said honestly. 'I haven't got a very big span—look.' She spread out her hands. 'Some of these chords will be beyond me.'

'Darling, you've only just got here, so don't start being defeatist already.' He spoke quite gently, but there was a faint undercurrent of irritation. 'I said I'd like you to have a look at the piece—try it over, that's all. I'm not planning to launch you on to the world stage with it next week.'

'I'll start on it tomorrow,' she said. 'I'm tired and a bit stupid this evening.'

'Then I recommend an early night.' He paused, then said rather carefully, 'I hope Magda spread the welcome mat for you, after all my groundwork.'

'She's been very kind,' Sandie said neutrally. 'I only hope I can be of some use to her.' She hesitated. 'The man who met me at the airport was—rather strange. He didn't seem to like me much.'

Crispin laughed. 'Well, don't lose any sleep over it, sweetheart. O'Flaherty likes very few people. He reckons he's descended from kings, and considers himself a cut above the rest of us. In actual fact, he's the gardener, handyman, groom and occasional chauffeur. So much for royalty!' He paused. 'But he's lived at Killane since the beginning of time, and he's Flynn's man, so unfortunately we have to tolerate him.'

'I see.' Sandie looked down at the keys. 'Someone said Flynn might be coming here. Are you sure he won't mind—having a guest he hasn't invited?'

There was a silence. Then, 'Flynn and I pursue a policy of non-interference in each other's lives, and preferably mutual avoidance,' Crispin said with forced lightness. 'So you really don't have to worry. Anyway, Flynn rarely comes within miles of the place when we're all in residence. He'll be in New York, or Tokyo, or somewhere. And when he does come, he retreats to his island.'

'His island?' Sandie questioned, her eyes going instinctively to the huge window, and the mist-shrouded water beyond.

Crispin nodded. 'It's at the far end of the lough—about as far from here as it's possible to get. He's built himself some kind of shack there, for when he feels like leading the life of a recluse.'

'Does that often happen?'

Crispin shrugged. 'Not often enough to suit me.' He gave her a rueful smile. 'I'm afraid Cain and Abel weren't the only brothers unable to get on with each other, although I don't think either of us have got near to contemplating murder, quite,' he added with a laugh.

'I—I'm sorry,' Sandie said with a slight awkwardness, not quite knowing how to respond to these family confidences. She decided to try a change of topic. 'You—you didn't tell me about the twins—they're real charmers.'

Crispin looked faintly surprised. 'I don't really see a great deal of them. They were my mother's "afterthought". She married Henri Clémence, the French polo player, but they split when the twins were still babies. They used to spend some time with him, but he married again a few years ago, and his second wife isn't so keen on having them around—so now they seem to be here more and more.'

'I see.' Sandie reflected that although Magda Sinclair had a large family, it seemed singularly disunited. It saddened her. As an only child, she'd always had a secret hankering for brothers and sisters.

'Now, I think the best thing for you to do is relax this evening,' Crispin was saying. 'And we'll get down to some serious work tomorrow, when you're rested.' He smiled at her, and his voice became husky. 'I seem to have been waiting for a thousand years for you to get here, Sandie.' He bent and kissed her on the mouth, his lips lingering on hers, persuading her to a sudden, heady response, as swiftly stemmed when she became aware of the gentle probing of his tongue, and, a little embarrassed, pulled away.

Crispin laughed softly, stroking a strand of pale hair back from her flushed face. 'My God, but you're so sweet,' he said wryly. 'It would be so easy to lose my head completely, but I'm not going to. I've made all sorts of good resolutions about you, darling, and I'm not going to break them this early in our relationship, so don't look so stricken.' He kissed her again, brushing his lips across her cheek. 'After all,' he murmured, 'we have the whole summer ahead of us to— learn about each other.'

He straightened, sending Sandie a smile which combined teasing with tenderness. 'Now, you'd better go and change for dinner. Magda's a bit of a stickler about punctuality—in other people.'

Sandie's legs were shaking under her, and her heart seemed to be performing strange tricks inside her ribcage, but she managed to make her way upstairs and find her room.

She closed the door and leaned against the stout panels, staring dreamily towards the window. Rain, homesickness and the ambiguity of her reception no longer mattered.

The whole summer, she thought—and Crispin. It was like some wonderful, incredible dream. And she hoped she would never waken.

*   *   *

Although she was so tired, Sandie found she was far too excited and strung up to sleep that night.

Crispin's words, and the promise they seemed to imply, echoed and re-echoed in her mind, as she lay staring into the darkness. Was it possible to fall in love so swiftly and completely? she wondered confusedly. Could he have found her, at that first encounter at the festival, so attractive that he'd been prepared to pull out all the stops in order to see her again? It seemed almost too good to be true.

Sandie shivered a little, wishing yet again that she had altogether more experience with men—that she knew more about life in general. It might help to plumb the emotional morass inside her.

Would she, she asked herself, ever have agreed to come to Connemara if she hadn't, in turn, been attracted to Crispin? Back in England, she'd rationalised it in her own mind as the kind of hero-worship usually reserved for film or pop stars—a kind of delayed adolescent crush, of which she'd been secretly ashamed. After all, she'd told herself, she was far too old for fairy-tales. Yet now, it seemed, incredibly, as if the fairy-tale might be coming true.

With a sigh, Sandie pushed back the blankets and eiderdown, and swung her feet to the floor. She had to do something positive to relax herself—switch her mind to a more tranquil path, or she wouldn't close her eyes all night, and would be fit for nothing in the morning—certainly not to undergo her first trial as Magda Sinclair's accompanist, which had been mentioned over dinner, or to make any attempt to play Crispin's *Elegy*.

She was still dubious about her technical ability to interpret the composition, but it was obviously important to Crispin that she tried at least, and she wanted to please him, so what choice did she have?

She put on her dressing gown and let herself quietly out of her room. The wall-lights were still burning as she made her way to the main gallery and looked over the banister rail down into the hall. The house was totally quiet, and clearly everyone was in bed, although there were lamps on downstairs as well. A deterrent to burglars, perhaps, Sandie thought, as she trod silently down the stairs, wondering if there could really be such a menace in this remote and peaceful spot.

The music room was in complete darkness as she let herself in, closing the door quietly behind her. Jessica had said the room was soundproof, and she hoped it was true. Music was the only way to relax herself, but the last thing she wanted was the rest of the household roused because of her own sleeplessness.

She would play safe by playing softly, she resolved. She walked to the huge window and stood looking out over the lake. The rain seemed to have eased at last, and a strong golden moon was in evidence between ragged, racing clouds, its light spilling across the restless waters.

Sandie caught her breath in delight. No need to think too hard about a choice of tranquilliser, she thought, as the first clear, gentle notes of Debussy's *Clair de Lune* sounded in her mind.

As she turned away to switch on the overhead light above the piano, her attention was caught fleetingly by another flicker of illumination moving fast on the other side of the lake. Car headlights, she realised, and at this late hour the driver was probably counting on having the road to himself.

She sat down at the keyboard, flexed her fingers, and began to play, feeling the tensions and doubts of the past twenty-four hours dissolving away as the slow, rippling phrases took shape and clarity under her hands. As she played, she became oblivious to everything but the mood of peace being engendered within her.

The last notes sounded delicately, perfectly, and were overtaken by silence. Sandie lifted her hands from the keys with a little sigh, and looked at the window for a last glimpse of the moonlight on the water. And saw with heart-stopping suddenness that she was no longer alone.

Reflected plainly in the glass was the tall figure of a man, standing motionless in the doorway behind her.

For a moment Sandie stared with fascinated horror, a hand creeping to her throat. Someone had broken in, she thought. All those lights left burning had been no deterrent at all—just a waste of electricity.

And even if she could summon up a scream, which was doubtful, as the muscles of her throat felt paralysed, who would hear it—from this of all the rooms at Killane?

'My God, I don't believe it!' His voice, low, resonant with a faint stir of anger just below the surface, reached her. 'I thought you'd have more bloody sense . . .'

A small choked cry escaped her at last, and she twisted round on the piano stool to face him, her last, absurd hope that it might after all, by some miracle, be Crispin seeking her out killed stone dead.

He took a swift stride forward, his face darkening with furious incredulity as they took their first full look at each other.

'Who the hell are you?' he demanded harshly. 'And what the devil are you doing here?'

'I could ask you the same.' Sandie got to her feet, stumbling over the hem of her cotton housecoat in her haste. 'Who do you think you are, breaking in here—frightening me like this?'

He was only a few yards away from her now, and far from a reassuring sight. He was taller than Crispin, she realised, and more powerfully built too, with broad shoulders tapering down to narrow hips, and long legs encased in faded denims. A thick mane of brown hair waved back from a lean, tough face, dominated by the aggressive thrust of a nose which had clearly been broken at some time, and a strong, uncompromising jaw. His mouth was straight and unsmiling, and his eyes were as coldly blue as the Atlantic Ocean in winter.

'Tell me who you are,' he said too quietly. 'Or do I have to shake it out of you?'

Sandie flung up an alarmed hand. 'Don't come any closer,' she said jerkily. 'I'm a guest in this house— a friend of the family.'

The wintry gaze went over her comprehensively. She saw his mouth curl with something like distaste.

'A friend of one member of it, I've no doubt,' he said cuttingly. 'As for being a guest, my good girl, I have no recollection of inviting you under my roof at any time.'

'Your roof?' Sandie echoed faintly. Oh, God, she thought. Not in Tokyo, or a thousand miles away, but right here, and blazingly angry for some reason she couldn't fathom. She swallowed. 'I—I think you must be Crispin's brother.'

'I have that dubious distinction,' he agreed curtly. 'And I'm still waiting for you to identify yourself, my half-dressed beauty.'

Sandie was quaking inwardly, but she managed to lift her chin and return his challenging stare. 'My name is Alexandra Beaumont,' she said quietly. 'And I'm spending the summer here having private piano coaching from Cris—Mr Sinclair.'

'So that's the way of it.' His tone held open derision. 'As an excuse, it has the virtue of novelty, I suppose.'

'It happens to be the truth.'

'And being down here, next door to naked, in the middle of the night, is part of the course, I presume.' He shook his head. 'I'm afraid, darling, that your— tuition is hereby cancelled. At any rate, it will have to continue elsewhere.'

'I don't understand.'

'Don't worry now. I'll make the situation clearer than crystal for you at a more civilised hour,' Flynn Killane told her with dangerous affability. 'It's altogether too late to be bandying words right now, so I suggest you take yourself off to whatever room you've been given.' He paused. 'I suppose you do have a room of your own?'

'Of course I do.' Now that she was over her initial fright, anger was starting to build slowly inside Sandie at this cavalier treatment. 'Look, Mr Killane, I don't know exactly what you're getting at, but...'

'Ah, well,' he drawled unpleasantly. 'Brains in addition to those blonde good looks would have been too much to hope for.' He went to the door and held it open for her. 'Now, on your way, Miss Beaumont, and try not to get lost in all those confusing passages.'

Sandie took a deep breath and tried to summon what dignity she had left to her rescue. But it was difficult when she was being sent to bed—just like a naughty child—and for nothing. *Nothing.*

As she walked past him, head high, Flynn Killane put out a hand and ran a finger down the broderie anglaise-trimmed neckline of her housecoat. Incredulously, Sandie felt his hand brush her breast, and recoiled, the breath catching in her throat.

'You look—very fetching.' The smile that did not reach his eyes was exactly the insult he intended it to be. 'You were no doubt hoping for company. What a pity your only visitor turned out to be myself!'

She said chokingly, 'Please don't expect a polite contradiction, Mr Killane. What I can't comprehend is how someone as kind and—and charming as Crispin can possibly be related to someone like you. Perhaps you really are some kind of changeling.'

She saw the lean face darken, and was aware of him taking one threatening step towards her. His hand closed on her arm, anchoring her, making retreat impossible.

He said softly, through his teeth, 'Now if you really want to make comparisons...'

He pulled her against the hard length of his body and kissed her on the mouth.

After Crispin's beguiling gentleness, Flynn Killane's cold-blooded, deliberately sensual exploration of her lips had the shock of an assault. For a moment Sandie was frozen, unable to credit what was happening, then she began to struggle wildly, her body twisting against his as she tried to free herself, and heard him laugh, deep in his throat. His hands slid down her body, moulding her slender contours through the thin fabric of housecoat and nightgown, and her whole being seemed to burn with shame at his touch.

For a long moment he held her, then, totally un-hurriedly, he lifted his head and released her, stepping back.

'Take that to bed with you, darling,' he said silkily. 'And while you're lying there, remember they're my sheets you're wrapped in.' He paused. 'Sweet dreams!'

She lifted her hand and slapped him as hard as she could across his tanned cheek, then she ducked her head, picked up the trailing skirts of her housecoat, and ran like a hare for the stairs and safety.

CHAPTER THREE

WHEN Sandie opened her eyes the next morning, the sun was shining into her room from a clear sky.

She sat up, aware of a faint throbbing in her temples, and pushed her hair back from her face. For a moment she felt totally disorientated, then, as the events of the previous twenty-four hours rushed back to confront her in their entirety, she sank back against the pillows with a little moan of dismay.

She glanced towards the window and the untrammelled blue of the skies, and winced. 'Hypocrite!' she muttered.

She knew an ignominious urge to stay where she was, with the covers pulled over her head, rather than have to get up and face the inevitable repercussions of Flynn Killane's unexpected return.

No wonder everyone had reacted as they had to her arrival if he was always as hostile and intolerant to people who were not there at his personal invitation! Yet surely someone of Crispin's eminence in the world of music did not have to go cap in hand to ask his half-brother's permission before inviting anyone to Killane.

Helpless colour flooded her face as she remembered the way Flynn Killane had spoken to her—the unequivocal inferences that he'd drawn from her presence. That had been quite bad enough without the appalling humiliation of that odious kiss.

It mortified her now to recall her own wistful fantasies about Crispin. It was as if a trail of slime had been laid across them, she thought, shuddering.

By this time, of course, everyone at Killane would know the owner of the house had returned. Flynn Killane was undoubtedly someone who could make his presence felt.

Sandie groaned and got reluctantly out of bed. Well, there was little point in delaying the inevitable.

Half an hour later, dressed casually but comfortably in her usual jeans and T-shirt, her hair twisted into one long braid, she went downstairs. It was essential, she thought, standing in the hall rather irresolutely, to find Crispin, and tell him what had happened.

As she paused, Steffie, followed by James, emerged from the dining room.

'Hello there,' Steffie was eating a thick slice of bread and marmalade. 'Do you want some breakfast?'

'I'm not very hungry,' Sandie excused herself hastily. The way her stomach was churning, it would be a miracle if she ever ate anything again.

James gave her a speculative look, then glanced at his twin. 'We're away down to the paddock,' he said. 'Why don't you come with us?'

Sandie hesitated. 'I think I'd better stay here.'

'I wouldn't,' Steffie said candidly. 'Flynn and Crispin are having a terrible row in the study, shouting their heads off. You're best out of it.'

'Crispin's doing all the shouting,' James supplied. 'Flynn's talking in that quiet, cold voice that I don't like.' He turned to Sandie. 'He wants you packed off back to England,' he informed her.

Sandie's heart sank. 'Oh, no! But why?'

Steffie giggled. 'Because he thinks you're Crispin's bit on the side,' she said airily.

By rights, Sandie should have administered some well-chosen reproof, but she was too angry.

'Well, he couldn't be more wrong,' she said curtly. 'And what business is it of his, anyway?'

'Oh, everything that happens at Killane is Flynn's business,' Steffie said sunnily. 'After all, it's his house, and Bridie says we're only here on—on suffrage,' she added doubtfully.

'Sufferance,' Sandie corrected automatically. But the twins were already heading for the front door, and after a moment's hesitation, she followed.

What an autocrat! she thought, smouldering. What a petty tryant—king of his rundown castle, and determined to let everyone know it!

She had hoped that by now Crispin would have explained the situation to him, and got him to see some kind of reason. She'd even imagined some kind of apology coming her way, and had planned how she would accept it with icy dignity. But it seemed she had totally underestimated the depth of animosity between the brothers. And because of it, there would be no second chance for her. She was going to be shipped back to England as if she was in some kind of disgrace, when she was innocent of everything but wanting to be a professional pianist—and a little wistful thinking about Crispin. And what was really so shameful about that? she asked herself defensively.

Flynn Killane was probably just jealous, she thought, her nails curling into the palms of her hands. He might be a top man in his field, but he had none

of the fame enjoyed by the rest of his family. Nor had
he anything like Crispin's good looks or charisma,
she thought. In fact, he looked as if he knew more
about street brawling than high finance.

The horses were already waiting at the paddock
fence for their visitors. Sandie joined in the ap-
portioning of carrot and apple, and other titbits, and
patted the velvet noses which came snuffling inquisi-
tively towards her.

'Do you want to come for a ride?' James asked.

Sandie shook her head. 'I don't think so. I've come
here to work—and to learn.'

'Well, don't expect a lesson from Crispin today.
He'll be slamming off somewhere in a temper like he
always does.' Steffie giggled. 'I love it when Flynn
comes home. There's always hell to pay!' She swung
herself athletically on to the fence, and on to the back
of the nearest horse, twisting her hand in its mane.

'You're not going like that. Aren't you going to use
a proper saddle—and a helmet?' Sandie watched in
alarm, as James also mounted bareback.

'Oh, we have them somewhere,' Steffie called back
over her shoulder as she trotted off. 'But Flynn says
we were born to break our bloody necks.'

For such a critic of other people's morals and behaviour, Flynn Killane's own remarks in the hearing
of his younger siblings could take some censoring,
Sandie thought with disapproval.

She turned back towards the house, and saw, her
heart sinking, that O'Flaherty was striding briskly
across the grass towards her.

'Himself wants to see you in the study,' he announced brusquely, adding, 'And at once will be just grand.'

Sandie toyed with the idea of sending back an equally curt message that Flynn Killane could go and jump in his own lake, but decided against it. Thrusting her hands in her pockets, she sauntered back to the house, with O'Flaherty in close attendance. Like some prison warder! she thought, seething.

The study was a pleasant room, its walls lined with books, and with a large, old-fashioned desk occupying pride of place. Flynn Killane was standing, looking out of the window. Without turning, he said, 'Sit down, Miss Beaumont.'

'I prefer to stand,' Sandie said, adding sarcastically, 'Isn't that what you're supposed to do when the headmaster sends for you?'

'Well, I'm no teacher of yours, thank God.' Flynn Killane walked to the desk and sat down casually on its corner. He was wearing close-fitting dark slacks today, and a white shirt, open at the neck, and with the sleeves turned casually back to reveal tanned forearms. 'I understand that's Crispin's role, and you're the eager pupil seeking enlightenment at the feet of the master.'

Sandie's lips tightened at the overt sneer. 'I don't know why you should find that so extraordinary. I can't be the first...'

'You're the first so-called student he's had the damnable nerve to bring here,' he returned tersely. He looked her over. 'I see last night's half-naked houri has been replaced by the well-scrubbed, youthful look,' he commented. 'Just who do you think you're fooling, Miss Beaumont?'

'This happens to be my usual appearance,' Sandie said icily. 'As for last night——' in spite of herself a faint flush rose in her face, '—I was not half-naked. I was perfectly decent.'

'I doubt if you know the meaning of the word.' The blue eyes were implacable. He leaned forward slightly, and Sandie found herself taking a hasty and involuntary step backwards—a move that she saw with chagrin was not lost on him. 'Let me give you some advice, Miss Beaumont. Get back where you came from, before any more harm is done.'

'Give me one good reason why I should.'

'Because no possible good can come of your remaining a day longer.'

'But I disagree, Mr Killane.' Sandie lifted her chin defiantly. 'Under Cris—Mr Sinclair's guidance, I intend to fulfil my potential as a pianist, and justify the faith he's shown in me.'

There was a silence, and Flynn Killane gave a meditative nod. 'Tell me,' he said softly, 'just how do you assess this—potential of yours?'

Sandie swallowed. 'I hope, one day, to be good enough to take my place on the concert platform.'

He laughed. 'And also, no doubt, to find gold at the end of some convenient rainbow.' He shook his head. 'That's so much moonshine, my girl. You're deceiving yourself.'

'What do you mean?' Sandie flung her head back. 'And what do you know about it anyway?' she added hotly.

He shrugged. 'In case you've forgotten, I heard you play last night.'

'And you think from that you can judge—you have the presumption—the gall to pass an opinion?' She was shaking with anger.

He looked faintly amused. 'I see that you've already been told about Flynn the Philistine,' he commented drily. 'Come on now, Miss Beaumont, I admit I don't play any kind of instrument myself. Neither do I lay eggs, but as someone once said, I know a bad one when I come across it.'

Sandie's lips parted in a gasp of pure fury, and Flynn Killane threw up a hand to stem the indignant torrent of words before she could give them voice.

'Not that I'd put you quite in that class,' he added. 'You play quite well—but you're not good enough to be a soloist in a million years, and both you, and certainly Crispin, must know that, so let's forget the cover story of burgeoning genius just waiting to be brought to fruition and get down to brass tacks.'

Sandie drew a quivering breath. 'You,' she said, slowly and distinctly, 'are the most hateful, obnoxious man I've ever had the misfortune to meet. You're utterly wrong about me, and everything about me. But I don't care about the kind of vile conclusions you've drawn. I know I've got what it takes, and with Crispin's help, I'm going to prove it.' Her voice shook, and she paused to steady it. 'I've come here to work,' she went on. 'Work—do you understand? Not—not to flirt with your brother. I have talent and I believe in myself. And nothing you say or do is going to make the slightest difference,' she added with a little sob.

He looked at her for a long moment, the blue eyes narrowed, then shrugged again. 'In that case,' he said, 'I'm sincerely sorry for you.'

'And I don't want your bloody sympathy either!' she snapped angrily. 'Oh, why did you have to come back—and spoil everything?'

'Put it down to natural perversity,' he said. 'You fight well, Miss Beaumont, although I enjoyed your struggles last night even more,' he added with an elliptical grin. 'But appearances, your own in particular, are against you. It's best you go back to England without delay, and I intend to make the necessary arrangements. You may not believe it now, but it's for your own good.'

The door behind them burst open and Magda Sinclair surged into the room. She was wearing a scarlet silk caftan this morning, lavishly embroidered with dragons, but the tartan scarf still protected her throat.

'Flynn darling,' she exclaimed, 'Crispin tells me you're planning to send this charming child away. But you can't—you simply can't!'

Flynn's expression suggested he was counting to ten very slowly. He said quietly, 'And why is that, precisely?'

'Because there's been some terrible misunderstanding,' Magda said earnestly. 'Sandie's come here for me—to take poor Janet's place—although why on earth she had to marry that man—but what's the use?' She paused. 'And this dear girl has given up her summer to help me instead. Isn't that sweet of her?'

'Sweet,' drawled Flynn, 'is not the word. There seems no end to Miss Beaumont's versatility. But I'm afraid you'll have to look elsewhere for your accompanist, Mother. The young lady is leaving us shortly.'

'Oh, but that's quite impossible,' Magda said swiftly. 'Why, it might take me weeks—months even—to find someone suitable. And darling Sandie's right here on the spot, and ideal for the job. I won't let you take her away from me.'

'That's nonsense, and we both know it.' Flynn was tight-lipped. 'Miss Beaumont is far from irreplaceable. Whatever Crispin may have claimed, there are better pianists around too.'

'But I like her.' Magda spread her hands dramatically. 'Oh, Flynn darling, sometimes you can be so—unkind—unthinking even. When I remember your beloved father—so sensitive to my every need.' Her eyes filled with sudden tears. 'How can I explain to you? I need someone who is *sympathique*. Someone I can get on with. Rapport between us is essential.' Her shoulders slumped dejectedly. 'But what's the use? You've never understood the artistic temperament.'

'Perhaps not, but sheer bloody-mindedness doesn't cause me too many problems,' Flynn said with a kind of weary anger. 'I don't need to ask who's prompted this little outburst.' He shrugged. 'Let Crispin have his way, then, as he usually does.' He went round and sat down behind his desk. 'And now, as we all have so much work to do, maybe we should get on with some of it.'

'Of course.' Magda's face was wreathed with smiles. 'I knew you'd see you were being the teensiest bit hasty over poor Sandie.' She took Sandie's arm. 'Come along, my dear.'

Sandie followed her to the music room, feeling slightly stunned.

She said quietly, 'I'm very grateful to you, Mrs Sinclair, and I'll try not to disappoint you.' She paused. 'I got the impression yesterday that you didn't really think I was suitable.'

'Well, that rather remains to be seen,' Magda Sinclair said briskly. 'But Flynn does tend to be rather overbearing in these matters, particularly where Crispin's concerned. And he'd done quite enough harm in that direction already. Now my boy deserves a little happiness.'

Sandie bit her lip. Her own private dreams were one thing, but she didn't want the rest of the household sharing Flynn's unpleasantly biassed view of what she was really doing at Killane.

She said awkwardly, 'I hope you don't think . . .'

'What I think is that it's time we got down to some serious practice,' said Magda, in a voice that brooked no argument. 'I've decided to add some traditional ballads to my usual repertoire for the autumn. You'll find a selection in that green folder in the end cupboard. We'll do some exercises, then run through a few of them—see what might be suitable.' She gave Sandie a firm smile. 'Now, let's start, shall we, my dear? The morning is nearly over.'

In retrospect, Sandie decided it was the most trying and demanding couple of hours that she had ever spent.

Crispin's hint that Magda was not always easy to get on with proved to be more than justified. She let Sandie see that her nervousness and lack of experience were severe irritants, and she made few allowances for either of them.

And because Sandie was so tense after that traumatic confrontation with Flynn, she found she was making more mistakes than usual—playing like an absolute tiro, she realised with dismay.

She could not be thankful that neither the sound of her struggles nor Magda's strictures could penetrate the walls of the music room, or Flynn Killane would have something to sneer about in earnest, she thought unhappily.

'Well, that was far from satisfactory,' Magda said at last, her face taut with displeasure. 'You are going to have to try much harder than that, my dear. Your sight-reading is poor in the extreme. I imagine your examiners have commented on it in the past.'

Sandie bent her head, staring down at the keys. 'No,' she returned despondently, 'it's usually quite good. I—I must be a little on edge.'

'Then I'd be grateful if you'd pull yourself together before our next session,' Magda said waspishly, and swept out of the room in a swirl of dragons.

Sandie knew an overwhelming urge to put her head down on the keyboard and bawl like a baby, before going to the study and asking Flynn Killane to put her on the next flight to England. But I won't give him the bloody satisfaction, she decided savagely, thumping out a few discords to relieve her mangled feelings.

Much to her relief, lunch was not a formal meal conducted *en famille*. Cold salmon and a variety of salads were placed on the sideboard in the dining-room, and people wandered in and helped themselves, buffet style.

The twins returned from their ride, mercifully intact.

'We're going for a swim this afternoon,' Steffie informed Sandie, helping herself lavishly to the strawberries and cream that formed the dessert. 'Do you want to come?'

Sandie shook her head. 'I don't think I'd better.'

'Well, you won't be wanted for anything else.' Steffie gave a giggle. 'Crispin's gone off in the car in a towering rage. He won't be back till this evening. And Mother always rests in the afternoon.'

'Come on down to the beach,' James put in. 'You may as well while you have the chance. O'Flaherty says it will be raining again tomorrow.'

'All right, then,' Sandie accepted, trying to hide swift disappointment. She'd wondered all morning where Crispin was. She'd needed desperately for him to reappear and give her self-confidence a boost. The fact that he'd apparently stormed off without even knowing whether she was to go or stay was something of a blow.

And it would undoubtedly be a relief to get away from the house and its pressures, she thought, and bit her lip. What a way to feel when she'd been there less than twenty-four hours!

But it would all have been so different if only Flynn Killane hadn't returned, she told herself passionately.

Oh, why couldn't he have stayed—a thousand miles away, as Jessica had said?

The twins found her a bicycle, and an hour later she found herself cycling with them down the narrow lane that led to the sea. The wind had dropped, and the sun felt warm on her back, and almost in spite of herself, Sandie's spirits rose. She felt more cheerful still when they arrived at the beach—a perfect crescent of pale yellow sand, sloping gently into the cream-edged blue of the Atlantic.

The twins threw their bikes down on to the short turf that fringed the sand, and charged off, leaving Sandie to follow more slowly, picking up the outer garments they'd discarded and placing them, folded, on a convenient flat rock. Like the twins, she was wearing her swimsuit underneath her clothes, and she peeled off jeans and T-shirt without haste. The sea looked cold, and it didn't disappoint her, but once she'd nerved herself to take the plunge she found the water refreshing and exhilarating.

James had brought a ball, and they played a noisy and cheerful game of 'catch', aiming the ball near rather than directly at each other to ensure maximum drenching.

Eventually Sandie called a laughing halt, and waded out to get her towel. She'd blotted the worst of the moisture from her shoulders and arms and was wringing out her hair when she heard the approaching sound of a horse's hooves. She glanced casually over her shoulder, then froze.

'It's Flynn,' James called out, quite unnecessarily. 'He's on Aran Lad. Don't they look grand together?'

Sandie was glad she was not expected to reply. The twins ran up to Flynn and jogged alongside, as he slowed the handsome chestnut gelding he was riding to a walk.

Sandie, scrubbing the towel wildly over her legs, sent him a fleeting glance, and saw with a kind of chagrin how much younger and more attractive he looked as he responded smilingly to the twins' excited chatter. He could be pleasant when he wanted to, it seemed.

Keep on walking, she prayed silently, as the gelding drew level with her. Oh, please keep going.

But he didn't, of course. As he reined the horse in, it tossed its head and executed a neat sideways dance. Sandie caught her breath, hoping against hope to see Flynn Killane being dumped on his arrogant head in the sand. But to her annoyance Flynn controlled his mount effortlessly, bringing it to a docile standstill.

Sandie, bitterly aware of him looming over her, made herself meet his gaze, and immediately wished she hadn't. Her swimsuit was conventional in the extreme, cut high on the hip, and square across her small, firm breasts, but the way he was looking at her, she could have been naked, she realised with a swift shock of embarrassment.

She'd never been deliberately mentally undressed by a man before, and helpless colour rose in her face as Flynn's eyes surveyed her with merciless and explicit sexual curiosity. She was tempted to snatch up the towel and hold it in front of her like a shield, but she suspected that any such move on her part would only cause him more cynical amusement, and refrained.

'Enjoying your afternoon of leisure, Miss Beaumont?' His voice was silky.

'More than I enjoyed this morning,' Sandie returned shortly, and he laughed.

'Really? So, my mother gave you a hard time, did she? Maybe Crispin should have warned you that when she picks up the cudgels on anyone's behalf, there's invariably a price to be paid.'

'Crispin wasn't around to warn me.'

'Well, that's another thing you'll have to accustom yourself to, darling, if you remain with us for any length of time. Crispin deals with his problems by running away from them.'

'Oh, I shall be staying, Mr Killane.' She gave him a defiant look. 'I thought that question had already been settled.'

'Don't count on a thing, Miss Beaumont.' He was smiling, but the note in his voice sent a prickle of tense awareness down her spine.

She said, 'It's hardly any wonder Crispin vanishes if you—persecute him like this.'

Flynn laughed. 'Persecute, is it?' he queried mockingly. He shook his head. 'Maybe I'm just trying to redress the balance of a lifetime of indulgence from Magda, in the first place, and a succession of pretty little blondes like yourself in the second.'

Sandie hoped she had concealed the pang his words had caused. She said curtly, 'Well, you can exclude me from that category, Mr Killane. As I've tried to make clear to you more than once, I'm here to work.'

'Of course. How could I have forgotten?' The blue eyes swept her mockingly once more. 'You're the very epitome of what a working girl should be.'

She bit her lip. 'I'd be in the music room at this moment, if you hadn't driven Crispin away.'

'I'll try and remember what a sensitive soul he is in future,' said Flynn. He gave her a last, derisive look, clicked his tongue to the horse, and moved off, breaking into an easy canter.

'Can't he just ride!' James said enviously, spreading out his towel and throwing himself down on to it. 'O'Flaherty says he could have been world class, better even than his father, if he'd stuck to it instead of commerce.' He sighed. 'We wish he'd come back here for good, don't we, Steffie? Then maybe he'd have us with him all the time.'

With a pang of sympathy Sandie remembered what Crispin had told her of the twins' background.

'But this really is your home, isn't it?'

The two exchanged rueful glances. 'Well, it is and it isn't,' Steffie said reluctantly. 'We're away at boarding school mostly, and sometimes, when Mother's touring, she arranges holidays for us with friends of hers—people who owe her favours—but we'd rather be here.'

'Only Flynn doesn't come as often as he used to,' James said mournfully. 'O'Flaherty says he gets sick, as who wouldn't, of having a decent house turned into a class of rehearsal-room.'

'Apart from the fact that he and Crispin hate each other,' Steffie added.

Sandie was aware she probably shouldn't be listening to all this, but found it quite irresistible.

She said tentatively, 'I suppose—your brother tends to feel the odd one out, with all this music?'

'It's not just that,' James said scornfully. 'Flynn and Crispin always fought like cat and dog, generally over women,' he added with a worldly air. 'Mrs Doherty from the gift shop says they were a pair of devils, always stealing and snatching each other's girls, and that nothing in a skirt was safe from them from here to Dublin.'

Sandie's brows drew together. 'I don't think we should be talking like this about your brothers' private affairs,' she said stiltedly.

The twins looked at each other and hooted. 'There wasn't much private about them. The world and his wife had them under discussion,' Steffie told her kindly. 'They'll be talking about you next.'

'Well, I'd prefer them not to,' Sandie said hotly. 'Besides, there's nothing to talk about.'

'Except that Flynn and Crispin have been bawling each other out ever since you got here.' James gave her an angelic smile.

'And I don't understand the reason,' Sandie said despairingly. 'Why does Flynn resent my being here?'

'Oh, he doesn't approve because of Francesca.'

'Francesca?' Sandie echoed slowly. 'Who is Francesca?'

The twins collapsed into paroxysms of mirth again.

'God, don't you know anything?' Steffie demanded between giggles. 'Why, she's Crispin's wife, of course.'

Sandie felt as if she'd been turned to stone. Crispin was—married? But it wasn't possible. She'd never heard any mention of a wife in any of the publicity about him. And if it was true, why hadn't he told her?

All at once the little secret dreams she'd been harbouring about him seemed not merely pathetic, but dangerous.

She drew a breath. 'I really shouldn't be letting you tell me these things. It isn't right...'

'Who's to hear us?' James asked practically. 'Anyway, you needn't consider us. We're used to broken homes round here.'

'And you don't have to worry,' Steffie added kindly. 'She and Crispin were always rowing at each other. In the end she walked out on him. She hasn't been back for two years, so he'll be about ready to fall in love again.'

'But you can't expect Flynn to be too pleased. Apart from anything, Francesca's parents still live over there at Croaig Mhor. And people round here still look down their noses at divorced people. Mrs Cadogan from the hotel says Mother is forgiven because she was widowed from her first true husband besides being a great artist, and judged differently from the rest of us.'

'Now look,' Sandie said with a touch of desperation as she digested all this, 'you mustn't get the wrong idea. I've come to Killane to—to play the piano, that's all.'

Another glance was exchanged and two heads nodded wisely. 'That's what Francesca used to say, every time she came over to the house. She was a pianist too,' said James, and grinned at her.

'In fact when you walked in yesterday, we all thought...' Steffie paused with a yelp, as James gave her a shrewd kick.

'Yes?' Sandie prompted rather tautly. 'What did you all think, precisely?'

'Oh, it doesn't matter,' Steffie mumbled after a pause. 'I think I'll go for another swim.'

It was clear the twins had decided they'd been indiscreet enough for one day, Sandie thought as she reached for her jeans. The sun was still blazing down, but she felt suddenly icily cold. She had to force herself to speak normally.

'I think I'd better be getting back to the house. I— I ought to practise ...'

'Can you find your own way?' James asked. 'We'll stay here for a while.'

'I'll be fine,' Sandie agreed hastily.

She was trembling as she cycled off, her mind dazedly trying to make some kind of sense out of what she'd been told. At least some of the question marks which had been hanging over her since she'd arrived at Killane had now been answered, but not in the way she'd expected or wanted, she thought forlornly.

And it explained some of Flynn Killane's hostility too, but not all.

What right has he to set himself up as some kind of moral arbiter on Crispin, anyway? she asked herself angrily. He's nothing but a hypocrite, if what the twins said is true.

Stealing and snatching, she thought, and grimaced. She couldn't imagine any woman in her right mind preferring a boor and a bully like Flynn to Crispin. And if Crispin made a mistake in marrying this Francesca, that surely doesn't mean he has to forfeit all future chance of happiness, she argued.

Flynn Killane seemed to be taking his self-assumed responsibilities as head of the house much too far. But he won't win, Sandie thought, lifting her face defiantly to the breeze. He won't spoil things. Because I won't let him.

And she shivered suddenly, as she was struck by the absurd conviction that—somewhere, somehow—Flynn Killane had heard her silent challenge—and accepted it.

CHAPTER FOUR

THE music helped, as it always did. As Sandie played, she felt her inner turmoil quietly subsiding as all her emotional concentration became centred on the notes she was trying to interpret.

Magda, she thought, would have nothing to complain of tomorrow.

As she played, she was marginally conscious of the panorama of lake and trees outside the huge window. The sight of the sun sparkling on the water seemed to calm and uplift her at the same time.

It was amazing, she thought, that someone as basically insensitive and—earthy—as Flynn Killane could have deliberately provided such an environment for the making of music, when it was something he didn't even approve of.

But then he was obviously a mass of contradictions, she decided with a shrug, and certainly not worth the amount of mental energy she seemed to be expending on him. But it was hard to dismiss him completely from her thoughts in the light of the twins' revelations, she told herself with an odd defensiveness.

And it was infuriating the way he kept intruding between her consciousness and the things that really mattered—like Crispin's *Elegy*, for example.

She took up it up and placed it on the stand, studying it frowningly, trying over a few of the opening chords. It was an amazingly complex composition, and far more technically demanding than anything she'd ever attempted in the past. But then Crispin had criticised her for being unadventurous, she thought with a mental shrug. Perhaps this was his way of launching her into the musical deeps.

She struggled with it for half an hour, then put it aside with a sigh, glad that he hadn't been around to hear her fumblings after all. But at the same time she couldn't help wishing that he'd stayed—given her his support—even explained exactly why Flynn was gunning for her.

Flynn again, she realised with total exasperation. And until she could dismiss him and his machinations from her brain, she was simply wasting her time here. She glanced at her watch and saw it was getting late. So it was probably best to call it a day, anyway.

She closed the piano and went up to her room to change for dinner.

'So there you are!' Crispin was standing beside the window. 'Darling, where on earth have you been? Bridie said you'd gone out somewhere with the twins.'

'I did—for a little while. We went swimming. But I've been back for ages—in the music room.'

'Well, it doesn't matter,' he said dismissively. 'Hurry up and change, my sweet, and I'll take you out for a meal.'

Her heart skipped a beat. 'I—I don't think that would be very sensible, in the circumstances.'

'What on earth are you talking about?' His brows drew together.

Sandie bit her lip. 'Crispin, why didn't you tell me you were married?'

'So that's it,' he said ruefully. 'My poor sweet, have you been worrying your head off about the fact that I have a wife somewhere? Because you really needn't, you know. Come out to dinner with me, and I'll tell you all about it.'

'Do you think we should?'

'Well, it will certainly be less wearing on the nervous system than eating here, and a damned sight more private,' he said shortly. 'I gather Magda worked a miracle and persuaded Flynn you were staying.'

'Yes, she did,' Sandie bit her lip. 'But I think she may be regretting it. Our—first session didn't go terribly well this morning.'

'Well, that was rather silly, sweetheart. Particularly when she's gone out of her way to help you.'

'I'm sorry,' Sandie said rather coolly, stung by the note of censure in his voice. 'But you weren't the only one to have—a traumatic interview with the master of the house today.'

Crispin sent her a repentant look. 'My poor girl! Was he a swine to you?'

'Yes,' she said baldly. She hesitated. 'Crispin, do you really think it was a good idea to bring me here—all things considered?'

'Darling, I didn't know Flynn was going to descend on us like a ton of bricks. He normally avoids the place like the plague when we're all here, and especially when I'm among those present. But you don't have to worry. He'll be gone soon, I promise.' He ran a smiling but at the same time critical eye over her casual attire. 'Now be quick and put on something pretty for me.'

Sandie noted with dismay that he showed no signs of taking his departure. Surely he didn't intend to stay in the room while she changed her clothes? Perhaps it was the kind of thing other girls took in their stride, but it was altogether too intimate a situation for her to handle this early in their relationship—especially when she didn't even know if there could be a relationship.

She said stiltedly, 'I'll—see you downstairs, shall I?'

His brows lifted. 'Turning me out, sweetheart? Well, I'll accept it this time—but you won't be shy of me forever, will you?'

She bent her head. 'I—I don't know. Crispin, I'm not sure what to think any more.'

Crispin smiled, brushing her heated cheek with a careless finger as he walked past her to the door. 'That's why I want to talk to you—alone, away from prying ears. I want to set the record straight, my sweet. So don't keep me waiting too long, will you?'

When she was alone, Sandie tore off her clothes with almost feverish haste, making her way along to the bathroom. Even if it meant keeping Crispin hanging about, she had to have a bath, and wash the salt out of her hair.

Half an hour later she walked sedately down to the hall. She was wearing one of her favourite skirts— huge jungle flowers in pink, turquoise and gold on a black background—and a plain black silky top, short-sleeved with a scooped neckline. Her hair still felt slightly damp, but she thought she looked good, and hoped Crispin would approve.

But it wasn't Crispin who was waiting at the foot of the stairs, his eyes fixed on her as she descended.

'"She walks in beauty like the night",' said Flynn, and managed to make it sound like an insult. 'Going somewhere, Miss Beaumont?'

'As a matter of fact—yes. If it's any concern of yours,' she added for good measure.

'I'm concerned with the welfare of everyone in this house,' he said. 'Even yours, my pretty fly-by-night. I suppose I don't need to ask whom all this glamour is aimed at?'

Sandie lifted her chin. 'You don't need to pry at all,' she said. 'But at least you won't be obliged to be civil to me over dinner.'

'Believe me, Miss Beaumont, I should have felt no such obligation.'

Her foot itched to kick him smartly on the shin, but common sense told her that she would make little impression against his riding boot, so she contented herself with a look of icy disdain before sweeping past him into the drawing-room.

'Nicely done.' His voice followed her sardonically. 'When the concert platform fails, you could always try the comedy stage.'

Sandie was still shaking inwardly with temper when she drove away from the house with Crispin ten minutes later.

'There you are,' said Crispin, pointing as they negotiated the narrow twisting road. 'As the song says, you can see the sun go down on Galway Bay, or very nearly. Another time I'll take you up on the Sky Road out of Clifden. The sunsets are spectacular from there.'

'O'Flaherty says it's going to rain again tomorrow.'

'Well, that could happen. One thing about the climate here, it's never dull.' Crispin paused. 'I hope you like seafood.'

'I love it.'

He laughed. 'A girl after my own heart!'

Sandie gave a constrained smile in response. She said, 'Crispin, shouldn't we talk—about Francesca?'

'Oh dear, that sounds terribly—and unnecessarily-serious.' His tone was still light. 'Save it for the restaurant, my sweet. I need all my attention to keep the car on what passes for a road round here.'

He took her to a hotel standing in its own grounds, the dining room windows looking over sloping lawns to the calm waters of the bay. Crispin ordered platters of Dublin Bay prawns and lobster, and a carafe of white wine, and when they'd been served, he said, 'Now, what's troubling you, my lovely Alexandra? The fact that I'm married—or simply that I didn't think to mention it?'

She summoned a smile, her fingers closing round the fragile stem of her wine glass. 'Both, I suppose. Perhaps I'm just being silly, only—I wish you'd told me.'

Crispin was silent for a moment, his brows drawing together in a frown. He said at last, 'I guess it didn't occur to me to say anything because I didn't think it mattered. It no longer does—to me. It's all over—an episode in my life I'm doing my best to forget.' His mouth tightened. 'I suppose Flynn told you, damn him to hell.'

The denial was on her lips, but she suppressed it. If Crispin was going to be angry, it was better his anger fell on its usual target, rather than the twins, she reasoned confusedly.

She said, 'It's not really important who told me. I just wish that it had been you.'

He looked at her ruefully. 'Call it a sin of omission. Or perhaps it goes deeper than that. Maybe I was afraid that if I told you I still had a wife—even if the marriage only exists in name—you might not have come here.'

Sandie looked down at the table, feeling the colour rise in her face. 'It's not really any of my business.'

'Oh, come on, sweetheart, you know better than that!'

Her heart began to pound in painful excitement, as it did whenever Crispin's voice took on that note of tender teasing. But there were other things she had to know before she could surrender to the hopeful joy inside her.

'Your wife—Francesca—she was a pianist too?'

'My former wife,' he said firmly. 'Yes, she had a career in music planned. That was one of the things that drew us together.' He drank some wine. 'And it was also the factor that drove us apart. Among other things.'

Sandie hesitated. 'Would you rather not talk about it? I'm sorry...'

'Don't be,' he said swiftly. 'They say confession is good for the soul, and maybe you're the ideal person for me to confide in, after all this time.' He paused. 'I met Francesca and fell in love, and for me it was as simple as that. I assumed it was like that for her too, but I was wrong. All the locals had always thought she'd marry Flynn and become mistress of

Killane, but he was far too busy playing the field, and never asked her. So in me Francesca saw the perfect way of getting her own back on Flynn, and boosting herself up the musical ladder at the same time. And I was too besotted to see it—then.'

Sandie swallowed. 'But that can't be all there was to it,' she protested. 'She must have cared for you.'

'Briefly, perhaps.' Crispin's mouth twisted. 'But it was a phase which soon passed. And it didn't help matters when she discovered that she didn't have what it takes to succeed as a soloist, and that my influence wasn't going to make the slightest difference. Somehow, that became my fault, along with the fact that she'd married the wrong man for the wrong reasons.'

Sandie stared down at her plate. 'That's—awful,' she said slowly.

'It was at the time, certainly. I still loved her—then. I wanted to try again—to fight for her, but she soon made it clear there was nothing left to fight for. In a way, it was a relief when she left me.'

'Do you know where she went?' Sandie's tone was hesitant.

Crispin laughed shortly. 'To pursue her career elsewhere, I presume. What does it matter? There was nothing for her to hang round for here. Flynn has no contacts in the music world, and she'd already got the message that he isn't the marrying kind—so...'

'But you're not divorced?'

He shrugged. 'She knows where I am if she wants to institute proceedings.'

'You'd think she would want to,' Sandie said, half to herself, and flushed when she caught his surprised look. 'I mean, having made the mistake, I'd want to put the whole thing right—start again.'

He reached across the table and took her fingers in his. 'But you, my sweet, are not Francesca. There's a warmth in you, a tenderness, and an intrinsic modesty about your talent which Francesca totally lacked, only I was too much in love to see it. She was a go-getter, ambitious down to her bones, hard as nails. In fact, she and my beloved brother were well suited to each other in those respects.'

'I wish he'd go,' Sandie said stormily.

'He will soon.' His tone was soothing. 'I've already told you, he doesn't stay around long. He's the eternal rover—always restless, looking for new worlds to conquer.' He smiled bitterly. 'And new women.'

Against her will, Sandie found herself remembering those few shattering moments in Flynn's arms that first night in the music room—the slow insolent rake of his eyes down her body on the sunlit beach only a few hours before.

She shivered. 'He's vile!' she said passionately.

Crispin smiled at her across the flowers and candles. 'And you're adorable,' he said softly. 'I should have waited for you to come into my life, little Alexandra, instead of chasing shadows.' He watched the warm colour rise once again in her face, and smiled. 'And you blush,' he said. 'I'd forgotten that women still could. Now eat your meal,' he added, releasing her hand. 'Unless my troubles have destroyed your appetite?'

She forced a smile. 'I don't think anything could do that. The food's wonderful.'

There was another pause, and she wondered if she'd said the wrong thing, but all he said was, 'So ethereal, and yet so practical,' before turning the conversation to the forthcoming concert season.

They lingered over the coffee and brandies, and Sandie was content, at least on the surface of her consciousness. Underneath, she was uneasily aware, there was a morass of tangled emotion, encompassing sympathy of Crispin, condemnation of the girl who'd treated him so callously, and violent resentment towards Flynn Killane.

A hazy moon hung over the trees as they drove back to Killane. Sandie felt reluctant to return to the house. It was no wonder that Crispin, sensitive as he was, felt the need to escape from it sometimes, she thought sadly. Flynn Killane had his island. Why didn't he go there and stay there, instead of sitting in judgement? He was the last person in the world with any right to criticise someone else's morals, after all.

'Are you coming into the drawing-room?' Crispin asked, as they entered the hall.

Sandie shook her head with a swift smile. 'It's been a wonderful evening, but I'm rather tired.'

'That's a pity.' He stroked the curve of her face with his finger. 'Because it doesn't have to end here—unless that's what you want.'

Her heart missed a beat, and her mouth was suddenly dry. She said falteringly, 'I don't understand.'

'Yes, you do. You knew from the moment we saw each other, just as I did. And we've become so close, darling, especially over the last few hours. I've told you so much—revealed for the first time all the hurt, all the loneliness Francesca left behind.' His voice was low, but it vibrated passionately. 'But you could heal me, little Sandie. Don't you know that?'

She didn't think she knew anything any more, she thought confusedly. Crispin was supposed to be her teacher, but now he wanted to be her lover. He'd promised he wouldn't rush her into anything, and yet within forty-eight hours of her arrival...

She found her voice. 'It—it's too soon.'

'How can you legislate about these things? I need you, sweetheart, and I think you need me. I want to know you in every way there is. I want to share everything with you—emotional and artistic fulfilment at their highest level. It could be a turning point in both our lives.'

Sandie drew a breath. 'Crispin—I don't know whether I'm capable of giving you what you want. I—I have to think about this...'

'Of course,' he said immediately. 'You're such a little innocent, my pet, that you're bound to have misgivings. But you must see that the closer we are in every way, the deeper the level of understanding we'll be able to achieve in our music as well as everything else. Maybe this is why you haven't quite come to terms with *Elegy* yet—because the passion in it defeats you. Because you've never experienced total fulfilment.'

Sandie bit her lip. 'Perhaps—I don't know.'

'How can you know?' He drew her into his arms. 'Let me open up this new world for you, my sweet. I want you so much.'

She remained passive while he kissed her, not encouraging the pressure of his mouth, the tentative probing of his tongue, but not rejecting it either. She had the uneasy feeling that if she responded too warmly, Crispin might try further intimacies, and her instinct told her she wasn't ready for that.

She detached herself gently from his embrace, and stood back. 'I really am tired, Crispin. I need to go to bed.'

'So do I.' His smile was rueful as well as tender. 'But I can see I'll have to be patient a little longer.' He looked down at her, his eyes searching. 'Or must I? Won't you take pity on me tonight, my sweet?'

She swallowed. 'I don't know—I can't think. I can't answer you now...'

'Then I'll postpone the question until later. But not much later.' He took her hands, lifting first one, then the other to his lips, then turned and walked away towards the drawing-room. Before the door closed behind him, Sandie heard Magda's voice raised in greeting and welcome.

As Sandie began to climb the stairs, she was aware that her legs were trembling. She felt torn apart by indecision. Her head might be advising caution, but her heart was thudding with nervous excitement. Crispin Sinclair wanted her—wanted to make love to her. Crispin, the rich, the famous, the supremely talented, actually needed her—Sandie Beaumont. Little Miss Nobody. She gripped the smoothly polished wood of the banister rail to convince herself that she wasn't dreaming, and paused for a moment to steady her breathing.

He had said they had both known from the first, but was that really true? She couldn't be sure. Yes, she'd been attracted to him, and flattered by his interest in her, she'd even thought in terms of falling in love, but had she ever anticipated a full-blown sexual affair with him?

I don't think it ever crossed my mind, she thought.

But there was so much else to take into consideration, she warned herself tremulously. For instance, she wondered if Crispin had paused to contemplate his mother's possible reaction to this fundamental change in their master-pupil relationship. Because she could not, in honesty, imagine Magda being particularly delighted with the news.

She still hasn't really accepted me as her accompanist yet, Sandie told herself, biting her lip. I still have a hell of a lot to prove. And I did come here to work.

As she reached the shadows at the top of the stairs, the landing light suddenly came on, and she recoiled with a faint gasp, blinking her eyes against the unexpected illumination.

'Well, he wastes no time, I'll give him that,' said Flynn. 'But before you become too flattered by his impatience, I should warn you it can work both ways. If you intend to test your power by stringing him along, you may well find yourself supplanted by a more willing lady, and to hell with the artistic rapport.'

He must have been standing there in the shadows—watching them, listening to every word, Sandie realised with blank horror.

She said chokingly, 'How dare you! Eavesdropping's a filthy trick!'

'But instructive, nevertheless. I'd never have thought of getting a girl into bed by telling her it would improve her piano playing.'

His tone was light, but its barely concealed note of contempt seared across her nerve endings.

'You're vile,' Sandie said tautly. 'And you couldn't possibly understand . . .'

'Of course not. A peasant from the bogs like myself shouldn't aspire to comprehend the tumultuous passions of genuine artists—even when they're just a thin disguise for old-fashioned lust.'

She bit her lip. 'I—I don't have to talk to you. It's none of your business anyway.'

'Oh, everything that happens at Killane is my business, as I've already told you,' he said softly. 'Even trying to talk some sense into a star-struck little idiot with her brains in her knickers.'

As her hand, instinctively, swept up, Flynn's fingers closed like a vice round her wrist.

'You don't play the same trick twice, darling.' His voice hardened. 'Not unless you want to invite the kind of retribution you'd least care for.'

'Let go of me at once!' She tried unavailingly to pull free.

'When I'm good and ready, and when you've listened to what I have to say.'

'Then say it and go to hell!' she flared.

'All right.' He paused briefly. 'If I thought there was a chance that Crispin would make you happy, then I'd stand back and let nature take its course. But he can't and he won't, and if you think you have a future with him, then you're fooling yourself because there's one woman in his life, and one only.' He released his grip on her so abruptly that she almost stumbled.

'Is that it?' Sandie rubbed her tingling flesh, glaring at him.

'It's enough to be going on with. If you want it more plainly, I'm telling you that Crispin's a married man.'

She said unevenly, 'I already know that. And I know all about Francesca too. Crispin has been perfectly frank with me—and I'm prepared to wait while it all gets sorted out.'

'Are you, now?' Flynn said derisively. 'Well, I doubt that he is.' He reached out and wound a strand of blonde hair round his finger, staring down at it with a faint grim smile. 'You have so many—irresistible attributes, Miss Beaumont.'

'You're—hurting me!'

'I'm trying to stop you from getting hurt, you little idiot.' He shrugged. 'But if you won't listen...' He smoothed the lock of hair back behind her ear and grinned down into her outraged face. 'In the circumstances, it would be tactless to hope that you sleep well, so I'll just wish you a pleasant night.'

'You're revolting!' she said stormily. 'You don't understand. You'd never understand anyone like Crispin.'

'I'll take that as a compliment,' said Flynn Killane. 'But I comprehend well enough what's going on in your head, my little frightened virgin. Because you are scared of this—step into the unknown, aren't you, darling? And although you're dazzled by all the fine words, you're still not sure whether Crispin's the man you want to take the step with. Whether he's capable of rousing you, until everything else in heaven and earth slips away. And you're right to have doubts. You deserve better.'

He was standing close to her—much too close, she realised, with a swift unwelcome thud of her pulses.

She said thickly, 'I suppose you mean yourself. Your conceit—your arrogance is disgusting!'

'Is it now?' said Flynn Killane. He bent his head, and his mouth brushed hers with swift, devastating sensuousness. As a kiss it could only have lasted a couple of seconds, no more, but she felt it in every fibre of her being.

Oh God, he wasn't even holding her, yet it was suddenly impossible to breathe—impossible to think. As he straightened, she found her lips forming his name, but whether in protest or plea, she was incapable of deciding.

He said softly and distinctly, 'Yes,' as if answering some unspoken question.

Then he turned on his heel and walked away from her, leaving her staring dazedly after him.

When Sandie reached her room, she was breathing as swiftly and painfully as if she'd taken part in some marathon. She slammed the door and leaned back against the heavy panels, trying to collect her thoughts and emotions.

She felt mortified to her very soul. She'd allowed Flynn to kiss her—although she couldn't see very well how she could have avoided it—and, although he'd barely touched her, she now had to admit that the caress had stirred her blood to tumult.

She shook her head slowly, staring unseeingly into space, rejecting the very notion. Flynn had just capitalised on a situation which Crispin had created. It was Crispin's words, Crispin's kiss which had aroused her, that was all.

She shivered suddenly. 'Stealing and snatching.' The twins' words returned to torment her. Flynn was simply trying to revive the old malicious sexual rivalry between his brother and himself, and she wanted no part of it. She dared not get involved, she realised.

He might be an unfeeling brute, but there was no doubt that Flynn Killane possessed a powerful sensual charisma, and knew how to use it. She wrapped her arms across her body in an unconsciously defensive gesture.

Well, in future she would be on her guard, and Flynn would be no further danger to her.

And in the meantime, there was Crispin...

She took a slow, deep breath, her eyes going almost distractedly to the big bed. He was going to come to her room later, she was sure of it, and then she would have to make one of the major decisions of her life so far.

She tried to imagine herself, undressed, lying in the bed in Crispin's arms, letting him kiss her—touch her—take her—and failed utterly. She wondered rather desperately if Crispin really appreciated how totally inexperienced she was. He'd talked indulgently about her innocence, of course, but at the same time she couldn't help remembering, incongruously, how impatient he became when she struck discords on the piano.

She set her teeth. Now she was just being silly. She tried to concentrate on practicalities. She hunted out the prettiest of her clean nightdresses and crept along to the bathroom for yet another quick bath. She sprayed herself with scent and brushed her long hair until her arm ached with the effort, all the time keeping a wary eye on her door, waiting for it to open, and Crispin to come to her.

She wondered if she ought to put on some lipstick. She applied some, then with a grimace, wiped it off with a tissue. But the stain of it still remained on her lips, and she supposed she should really have another wash. She was half-way to the door when she stopped suddenly, her hands clenching into fists at her sides.

What the hell was she doing? She was running in fruitless circles, like a hamster on a wheel, just trying to stop herself from thinking—from considering too deeply what she was doing.

She had been listening, she realised, for the telltale footstep in the passage outside not with eagerness but with dread. Because, although it galled her to admit it, Flynn Killane had been right about one thing. She wasn't sure. In fact, she was a mass of seething doubt. She had more or less allowed Crispin to talk her into something she just wasn't ready for. She couldn't take this giant leap in the dark—surrender herself without commitment, especially in this house where all his family lived.

It's impossible, she thought, pressing her hands frantically to her face. What could he have been thinking of? And why did I give him even the slightest idea that I would be willing?

She half stumbled to the door, and using both hands, turned its big old-fashioned key, screeching in protest, in the lock.

She turned off the light and got into bed, pulling the covers up to her chin, hoping desperately that when Crispin came knocking at her door, he would simply think she was asleep, and go away again. She prayed he wouldn't actually try the door, and discover the reality of her rejection of him.

It would be awful trying to explain it to him, trying to justify her change of heart, if that was what it was. Whereas tomorrow she could talk to him rationally, explain her misgivings—his own word. But it was deeper than that. She'd experienced something close to panic. She needed more time, and more reassurance. Surely—surely she could make him understand.

She lay still, staring through the darkness at the door, as the minutes became hours, and until, eventually, weariness overcame her, and she fell deeply asleep.

CHAPTER FIVE

SANDIE slept late the next morning. When she finally woke, a glance at her watch had her frantically scrambling into her clothes. When she arrived downstairs, out of breath, and a little embarrassed, the house seemed curiously quiet.

'So there you are,' Bridie appeared from the kitchen regions. 'I suppose you'll be wanting coffee.'

Sandie hesitated. 'I'm not sure I'll have time. Mrs Sinclair will be wanting me.'

'She's gone into Galway with the young ones. They'll not be back until teatime.'

In a way it was a relief. Sandie felt as if her head was stuffed with rather painful cotton wool, and not at all in any state to cope with Magda's strictures.

She nerved herself. 'Do you know where Mr Crispin is?'

If he'd come to her room last night, she would been totally oblivious to the fact. But whatever had happened, they had to have a serious talk.

Bridie laughed. 'Mr Crispin, is it? You'll not be seeing him before noon, with the head that he'll have on him! I'll get your coffee. Will you take a rasher with it?'

Sandie shook her head. 'Just some toast would be fine.'

'Toast!' Bridie scoffed. 'Why, a puff of wind would blow you away entirely!'

She went off, muttering under her breath, and Sandie walked slowly into the dining-room. Jessica was seated at the table, frowning over an article in the *Irish Times*.

She gave Sandie a brief smile. 'Hello, there. You've been let off the hook today.'

'So I hear.' Sandie pulled out a chair and sat down. 'Is—is Crispin ill?'

His sister's smile widened. 'Not unless they classify hangovers as diseases these days.'

'A hangover?' Sandie's eyes widened. 'But he didn't have that much to drink at dinner.'

Jessica laughed. 'Who's talking about dinner?' she demanded. 'It was what came after. Flynn challenged Cris to a quick snooker match. In the end, it lasted half the night, and a lot of Black Bushmills, most of which seems to have been swallowed by Cris, because Flynn's fresh enough this morning.'

Sandie found her hands curling into involuntary fists in her lap. She said slowly, 'I—see.'

And she did see, only too well. The lord and master of Killane had chosen to intervene yet again, even though his interference was unjustified and totally unnecessary.

How dared he? Sandie raged inwardly. Oh, God, how dared he?

She dismissed the fact that the last thing she'd wanted the previous evening had been a visit from an amorous Crispin. She'd made her decision about that, and been prepared to carry it through, however awkward the consequences.

Flynn Killane had no right to assume that she was willing to go along with Crispin's advances. His attitude was arrogant, overbearing and insulting. She could handle things for herself.

It wasn't even as if he'd done it for the best possible motives—for her protection. She knew quite well that it was simply and crudely to put a spoke in her wheel.

'Is something wrong?' asked Jessica. 'You look a bit jaded too. I hope you're not coming down with something. Magda has this morbid fear of people with colds.'

Sandie forced a smile. 'No, I'm fine. I was just wondering what to do with myself, after I've had my practice.'

'Well, you could always take Kelly for a walk.' Jessica indicated the spaniel, who was sprawled asleep in a patch of sunlight near the window. 'Magda bought him as an excuse to take exercise herself, but you can guess how long that lasted,' she added, grinning. 'Each time the wind changed she foresaw laryngitis. Anyway, if you're going out, I'd go soon. This weather isn't going to last.'

'I must get some work done first,' said Sandie. 'After all, that's what I'm here for.'

'Whatever you say,' Jessica said equably, and returned her attention to her paper.

The practice session was hopeless, Sandie was forced to admit after an hour and a half. She was just too angry and upset to make any proper progress. She could not dismiss Flynn and his overbearing behaviour from the forefront of her mind, try as she might, which was infuriating in itself. Because the last thing she wanted or needed was to think about that—boor.

She closed the lid of the piano with a muted slam, and rose. She would simply have to do as Jessica suggested, and walk off her ill-temper with Kelly.

The spaniel seemed delighted at the prospect of a walk. Sandie took the leash she found hanging in the porch, but didn't attach it to the dog's collar, as Kelly seemed perfectly happy to gambol along beside her.

She turned inland, forsaking the road as soon as possible for short springy turf and bracken, heading for the lower slopes of a tall hill which just seemed to have missed being a mountain. The sun was warm on her back, and the air smelled clean and fresh. She drank it in by the ecstatic lungful.

Connemara had so much to offer, she thought, watching the changing shadows on the sunlit slopes as fleecy clouds drifted overhead. She had never seen so many shades of green in any landscape, and the tops of the Twelve Pins were a misty indigo.

If it weren't for Flynn Killane, life would be perfect.

Well, not completely, she was forced to acknowledge on reflection. There was still the existence of Crispin's marriage to take into account. She was vaguely troubled by the fact that he'd made no move to dissolve the marriage himself. Surely if Francesca had walked out on him two years previously he was legally entitled to do so, instead of waiting for her to make the first move.

Unless Irish law was different. But Crispin wasn't Irish, so probably it didn't apply to him anyway.

She shook her head, feeling totally confused. There was no reason for her to be considering this anyway. It wasn't as if Crispin had asked her to marry him. In fact she wasn't sure whether she was included in his long-term plans at all. Perhaps all he had in mind was a summer of sex at Killane, and then goodbye.

What she had to decide was, if that was all that was on offer, would it be enough?

She shivered slightly, looking round for Kelly, suddenly aware that the scudding clouds from the west weren't quite so beguilingly fleecy any more, but greying and solidly packed. She called the dog's name and whistled, but there was no responding bark. Clearly Kelly had taken advantage of her abstraction to go on some exploration of his own, and was not to be distracted.

Oh, hell, Sandie thought, casting an apprehensive glance at the sky. She stood still, staring round her for betraying signs of movement. A few isolated sheep and cattle were grazing, completely untroubled, so Kelly couldn't be in their vicinity.

Where's he gone? she groaned inwardly. I should have kept him on the lead, I suppose, but he seemed so well behaved. I'll have to find him.

She unslung the sweater she was wearing round her shoulders and put it on, although it would be little enough protection against the rain which was threatening with every minute.

Sandie couldn't believe conditions could change so quickly—or a spaniel vanish apparently off the face of the earth. He must have found some damned rabbit hole, she thought crossly. I hope he hasn't got stuck.

She walked on slowly, calling and whistling until she was nearly hoarse. She was getting really worried now. Kelly wasn't just an agreeable companion, he was a valuable dog, and she had lost him.

I'm going to be *persona non grata* with every member of the household at this rate, she thought forlornly, as the first cold spatter of raindrops hit her.

She could see the end of an enormous pipe, clearly used for drainage, protruding from the ground, and she made her way towards it. She called 'Kelly!' again, and wondered if she had really heard the echo of a faint bark from somewhere deep in the pipe's interior or whether she was just imagining it. She looked inside the pipe, her mind quailing at the prospect of crawling along it, even a little way.

Oh, Kelly, she wailed silently, please come back!

It was raining more heavily than ever. The wind had risen, and seemed to be driving the water at her almost horizontally. Within minutes she was soaked. She turned and began to run with a certain amount of care back towards the road, head bent miserably, her soaked trainers squelching. After all, the last thing she wanted at this stage was to slip, and maybe sprain her ankle.

Feeling more wretched by the moment, she gained the tarmac and began to jog through the puddles, heading back towards Killane.

She'd gone about half a mile when she heard the sound of a car engine coming up behind her, and stepped to the side of the road, her hand raised to beg a lift. Please stop! she implored silently.

To her relief the estate car was already slowing. It halted beside her, and the passenger door swung open.

'Fancy meeting you here,' Flynn Killane said softly, his glance deriding her bedraggled appearance.

Sandie could have jumped up and down screaming. She had the most appalling luck, she thought dismally. Of all the people in the world, why did he have to come along?

She was strongly tempted to slam the car door and continue walking.

'Don't be a fool,' he said shortly, as if she'd spoken the thought aloud. 'Now get in before you catch pneumonia.'

Seething, she obeyed, sitting bolt upright in the passenger seat and staring defiantly ahead of her through the rivulets of water running down the windscreen.

Flynn gave a faint sigh. 'Now listen to me,' he said. 'I can stand you damp, I can stand you resentful, but the two combined are more than flesh and blood can bear. Shall we declare a temporary truce for the duration of this journey? After all, I didn't have to stop.'

She wanted to tell him stiffly to go to hell, when suddenly the sheer ridiculousness of the situation struck her, and she felt a reluctant giggle surfacing inside her. She suppressed it instantly.

She bit her lip. 'I suppose we'll have to.'

'I'm glad you haven't overwhelmed me with gratitude,' he said drily as he put the car in gear. 'And as we're actually conversing, could you tell me why you're clutching that dog lead, with no dog in sight?'

'I took Kelly for a walk.' Her voice wobbled defensively. 'But he ran off somewhere and I've been hunting ever since, but I can't find him anywhere, and I've called and called...'

'Don't worry your head,' Flynn advised. 'The beast will be safe and snug at Killane at this moment. He hates the rain, and the moment he smells it, he makes for home.'

'I see,' Sandie said in a stifled voice. 'I wish someone had told me.'

'Well, we all know his little ways. I suppose it never occurred to anyone to warn that you'd probably be coming home alone.' He paused. 'While we're on the subject of being solitary, I hope Crispin's failure to appear last night wasn't too grave a disappointment for you.'

His voice was silky, and Sandie flung him a fulminating glance.

'Not in the slightest. I wasn't actually expecting him, and I have no intention of having an affair with him.'

'Very commendable,' said Flynn. 'But did it occur to you that Crispin's expectations and intentions might have been very different, and that the choice might not have been yours?'

Sandie stared down at her fingers, interlaced together in her lap. 'I certainly didn't think he'd be prepared to break my door down, no.'

'You locked yourself in?' The surprise in his voice needled her afresh.

'Yes, I did,' she said tautly. 'I'm not the pushover you seem to think, Mr Killane, and I do have my own ethical code, which does not include having an affair with a married man, whether you believe me or not.'

'You sound very rational and moral in the cold light of day,' Flynn commented. 'Last night your decision didn't seem nearly so cut and dried.'

'That still doesn't mean I needed you to make it for me,' she said angrily. 'I could cope.' She paused. 'I suppose you think you've been very clever.'

'I was quite impressed by my reading of Crispin's psychology, it's true,' he said calmly. 'I reckoned the only factor which could take precedence over this planned seduction would be the prospect of his scoring a swift victory over me at snooker. He's never managed it yet, and it maddens him beyond bearing. He's also under the illusion that the more he drinks, the better he plays,' he added with a faint shrug. 'I had to put him into his own bed at three this morning.'

'You, of course, remained stone cold sober.'

'I make no such claim. But I was in better shape than Crispin.' He slanted a sidelong grin at her. 'I was half tempted to come and seduce you myself.'

Sandie bit hard on her lip. 'If you want to maintain this truce I'd be glad if you didn't make remarks like that,' she said, forcing her voice to remain steady. 'I don't find them even remotely amusing.'

'What makes you think I was joking?' His tone was still light, but there was a note in it which held danger signals.

The palms of Sandie's hands were suddenly damp. 'Because you can't possibly be serious,' she returned. 'We don't even like each other, Mr Killane. We've clashed at every opportunity since the first moment we met.'

'And you don't think that bed might be the ideal place to reach some kind of settlement? Passion and hate are close kin to each other, after all.'

'But I don't hate you,' Sandie said coldly. 'I merely dislike you. And I'd be glad if we could change the subject. This one is distasteful. In the meantime, while I'm at Killane, I shall continue to keep my door locked.'

'A very virtuous resolution,' he said mockingly. 'But there are three things you haven't taken into account.'

Her fingers tightened round each other. 'I'm sure you're going to tell me what they are.'

'Firstly, as owner of Killane, I could have a master key to all the rooms. Secondly, if I wanted a woman, no old rusty lock would keep me out anyway. And thirdly——' he paused.

'Well?' Sandie prompted icily, despising herself, as the silence lengthened.

'Thirdly,' said Flynn, 'I could stop this vehicle here and now, and persuade you to change your mind. And we both know it.'

Her breathing was ragged. 'That is—not true.'

'Oh?' Flynn began to brake quite gently. 'Shall we put it to the test?'

'No!' Sandie's voice cracked in something like panic. 'Oh, no—please!'

A smile twisted the corner of his firm mouth. 'I thought not.'

Sandie shrank into the corner of her seat, acutely aware that her skin seemed suddenly burning under her damp clothes.

Flynn sent her another sideways glance, then, to her thankfulness, remained silent until the car drew up at Killane's front door.

'In with you,' he directed briefly. 'I recommend a hot bath, and some whiskey, if Crispin's left any.'

She said in a stifled voice, 'Stop telling me what to do,' and fled precipitately into the house, and up to the room which now seemed, at best, only a fragile refuge.

*　*　*

Although it galled her, she took the first part of Flynn's advice and soaked herself in a hot tub before vigorously towelling her skin and hair until her body glowed and her scalp tingled.

But nothing could dispel the small dark shiver, deep within her, which Flynn's words had engendered.

The fact remained that, although it shamed her to her soul to admit it, she could not risk being in his arms again, and that he was aware of this. In spite of his remarks, she did not believe he would ever take advantage of the situation. It was enough that he could torment her with it.

And she knew, as well, that if Crispin's caresses had aroused anything like the same response in her, she would not have locked her door.

Yet it's Crispin that I really want, she thought achingly. Dear God, it's all such a mess!

When she got back to her room, she saw with disfavour that the treacherous sun was shining even more brightly than it had earlier. She heard the gong sound for lunch, but decided to ignore it. She was hungry, but there was every chance that Flynn would be present at the meal, and she didn't want to face him again just yet.

She waited until the coast was clear, then made her way to the music-room. This time she wasn't going to let any tangle of emotion get between her and some serious work, she told herself firmly. She and Crispin might never be lovers, but she could still be his star pupil. She could still make music her life.

She began with the usual scales, repeating them until her fingers moved with the desired smoothness and rhythm over the keys. Then she turned to the sonata

Crispin had prescribed, and plunged into the scherzo. It was a tricky piece, and her first attempt at it had been unimpressive, but today she played it without stumbling. It still wasn't good, but it was an improvement. She picked up a Chopin nocturne next, indulging herself because it was one of her favourites, feeling, with relief, the tension inside her relaxing at last.

And then, almost before she realised it, her fingers strayed into *Clair de Lune*.

There'd been no sunlight sparkling and dancing on the water the last time she'd played it, she thought, and no boat with a furled blue sail, tied up at the small landing stage just below the window.

She'd been on edge that night too, she remembered, but with happy excitement. She'd had no idea what was awaiting her. The sharp disruption which was about to enter her life.

She sighed, bringing her hands down on the keys in harsh discord. I won't think about him, she told herself vehemently. I won't! It's Crispin I should be considering.

She took down the *Elegy* and tentatively tried the opening chords. She had the oddest conviction that if she could overcome her crisis of confidence about the work, everything else in her life would fall into place as well.

The trouble is I want it to happen here and now, she told herself wryly. And it's not going to be like that.

The drawing room was deserted, when Sandie arrived there for tea, except for Kelly, who wagged a placatory tail when he saw her, from his position on the hearthrug.

'You wimp!' Sandie bent to fondle his ear. 'I thought spaniels liked water.'

He gave her a derisive look, and relapsed into a deep sleep.

Sandie helped herself to soda bread and thick homemade strawberry jam, and carried them to the window seat. The sun was pouring in through the panes, and she flexed her shoulders gratefully in its warmth. She couldn't deny that in spite of her bath, she felt a little shivery.

Perhaps water didn't suit her either, she thought, and gave a deafening sneeze.

'Good God!' Magda said sharply from the doorway. 'Are you getting a cold?'

Sandie looked up with a start. 'Oh, hello, Mrs Sinclair.' She tried a smile which was not returned. 'Did you have a good trip to Galway?'

'Shopping for children is always a bore,' Magda said dismissively. 'And I asked you a question, Alexandra.' Her hands went up to rearrange the inevitable scarf round her throat. 'Because if you are catching a cold, I must insist you stay in your room until it's over, my dear. I cannot risk infection of that kind.'

Sandie gaped at her. She was about to say, 'You can't be serious,' when she remembered what Jessica had said earlier, and it was borne in upon her that Magda meant every word.

She said, 'I did get caught in the rain this morning, but I'm sure it's nothing serious.'

'Well, we can't take any chances,' Magda said with determination. 'My throat is so vulnerable. You'd better go and lie down, and if your chill develops, I'll send for Dr Grogan tomorrow.'

'But I'm not ill.' Sandie didn't know suddenly whether to laugh or cry. 'And I really don't need a doctor.'

Magda gave her a minatory look. 'Not for you, dear child. For me—preventive medicine. Run along now. I'll tell Bridie to serve your dinner in your room.'

'But my work——' Sandie put down her empty plate, aware that her hands were shaking. 'I can't abandon my music for—a hypothetical infection that might never develop!'

'A rather self-centred attitude, my dear. You have to understand that there are other priorities.'

'Mrs Sinclair,' Sandie said desperately, 'please be reasonable...'

'Reasonable?' Magda interrupted, her brows rising in hauteur. 'I think you forget yourself, young woman. Now please don't argue any more.'

'What's going on?' Crispin asked peevishly as he walked in. Sandie's heart lifted, then sank again. He was very pale, and there were taut, ill-tempered lines around his eyes and mouth.

'Alexandra has a virus,' said his mother. 'I have been trying to impress upon her the importance of adopting some kind of quarantine until the danger of it spreading has passed. But I'm afraid she's not being very co-operative.'

'One sneeze,' Sandie protested defensively, horribly aware that another one was welling up at that very moment. She braced herself against the expected explosion, but it faded, leaving her with watering eyes.

'Oh, for God's sake!' Crispin poured some tea, and stared at it with loathing. 'If it's not one damned thing, it's another. What with Flynn's bloody meddling, life is sheer hell at the moment!'

Sandie bit her lips. 'I'm really sorry about that. Perhaps we—we should talk . . .'

'Well, not now, there's a good girl,' he said dismissively. 'I've got other things on my mind.' He turned to his mother. 'Do you know what he's done?'

'He mentioned it.' Magda put a hand on his arm. 'Darling, perhaps he meant it for the best. After all, it's a difficult situation. You must see that.'

Sandie felt herself going hot and cold all over. They were talking about her, about last night, she thought with horror. It must be common knowledge.

'I think you need a breathing space—time to reflect,' Magda went on, her voice throbbing with emotion. She paused. 'That's why Alexandra's cold seems so—opportune. It would avoid—complications at the moment.'

'You could be right.' Crispin swung to Sandie, giving her a smile that did not reach his eyes. 'Darling, if you are getting a cold, then bed's the best place for you—you must see that. You can't simply pass it to the rest of us. It would be disaster.'

Sandie stared at him in disbelief. She'd counted on his support in making Magda see sense.

'But I may not even have a cold,' she began, only to be interrupted sharply by Crispin.

'Well, let's not take unnecessary risks, my sweet. You're looking like a ghost as it is. A few days' cossetting won't do you any harm at all. Now let's have no more argument,' he went on decisively, as Sandie's lips parted in futile protest. 'You go upstairs, and I'll get Bridie to concoct one of her famous toddies for you.'

'There's no need to bribe me!' Sandie knew an overwhelming urge to burst into tears. 'I can see I'm fated to stay in my room, whatever I say. I wonder what you'd do if I had—German measles. Put me on the first plane back to England, I suppose.'

'Now don't be difficult, sweetheart.' There was annoyance underlying the coaxing note in his voice. 'It's a house rule, I'm afraid. People with colds don't spread them around.'

But it isn't just that, Sandie thought as she made her way to the door. All that talk about a breathing space means Magda doesn't want us to get involved, and that's really why I'm being banished.

Crispin's attitude seemed to convey that he was having second thoughts too, and this was vaguely hurtful, although it shouldn't have been, Sandie admitted to herself as she stood, irresolute, in the hall. Logically, she should have been relieved, but it was aggravating that she hadn't been given the chance to express her own views. And, even worse, she'd been left with the impression that Magda felt she was trying to trap Crispin in some way.

And I'm not, she thought angrily. He was pressuring me.

She took one step towards the stairs, then stopped, stamped her foot, and swung round, making instead for the open front door, and the garden beyond. I won't be sent to my room as if I was a naughty child, she thought rebelliously. it's quite ridiculous. This is a total madhouse!

She heard the sound of footsteps on the gravel outside, and dodged swiftly into the open dining-room doorway. The last thing she wanted was someone else telling her to go to her room. She heard the sound of the doorbell echoing through the hall, and then a girl's voice, low and attractive, calling, 'Is anyone there?'

Surprised, Sandie permitted herself a cautious peep round the door.

The girl stood in the doorway. She was tall and slim, wearing cream pants and a matching shirt, and her long blonde hair, gleaming in the sunlight, spilled over her shoulders and down her back.

For one crazy moment Sandie thought she was looking in a mirror. It wasn't just the hair—it was the violet eyes, the shape of the face too. She felt as if she'd frozen, turned to stone.

She didn't need Bridie's glad cry of, 'Miss Francesca, is it yourself at last? Welcome, darling! Welcome back where you belong,' to tell her the newcomer's identity.

The girl's smile was rather sad. 'Is it, Bridie? I'm not so sure about that.'

As the two of them walked down the hall towards the drawing-room, Sandie wanted to shrink further into her self-imposed sanctuary, but she was incapable of movement. A whole lot of things had become suddenly and brutally clear to her. She knew now why her appearance had been such a shock to everyone. It explained Flynn's first angry reaction that night in the music room.

We're the image of each other, she thought with horror. And everyone knew it but me.

It was agony waiting there in the dining room for Francesca to be ushered into the drawing-room with due ceremony, and for Bridie to take herself off back to the kitchen, dabbing her eyes on her apron.

As soon as the hall was clear, Sandie put her head down and dived for the door. She had no very clear idea where she was going, or what she was going to do. She only knew she had to get away from the house.

Instinct told her to avoid the side of the house where the drawing-room was situated. Arms wrapped round her body, throat constricted and eyes smarting, she flew across the side lawn, bypassed Magda's formal rose garden, and found herself on a path she'd never taken before.

The path sloped downwards, and ahead of her she saw the gleam of water, and realised this was the way to the lake. For a moment she hesitated, then, with a mental shrug, she plunged down towards the landing stage.

She was shivering violently when she got there, but told herself this could be explained by her fraught emotional state. The breeze off the water had an edge to it too, belied by the brightness of the sun. But then everything at Killane was a lie.

She walked over to the edge of the landing stage and stared down at the glittering water, its sparkle intensified by the unshed tears pricking at her eyelids. How could she have been such a blind, gullible fool? Why hadn't she made proper enquiries—insisted on an explanation? Her hands clenched into painful fists.

They must all have been laughing at her—or pitying her, and she wasn't sure which was worse.

She thrust her hands into her pockets and trod restlessly along the planking to the boat she had noticed from the music room, and looked down at it listlessly. There was a small, neat cabin, she saw, and an auxiliary engine, yet the boat was compact enough to be handled by a single occupant. She had to admire its trim lines, and the spotless gleam of its brass and paintwork, the name *Graunuaille* being picked out on the bow in gold.

Flynn had his own means of escape, she thought enviously. Whereas she would have to undergo the humiliation of making her presence known to Francesca Sinclair, and hope that someone would take her to the airport, so that she could go back to England and lick her wounds in peace.

'Going for a sail, or planning to drown yourself?'

Sandie turned, her heart thumping, to find Flynn had emerged unnoticed from the boathouse and was standing watching her, his face enigmatic, his hands resting lightly on his lean hips.

She said huskily, 'You know, don't you? You know what's—happened?'

'I can guess,' he said. 'Francesca has come to visit, and you've seen her, and drawn certain conclusions.' He shrugged. 'It was inevitable.'

'Is that all you have to say?'

'I tried to warn you—to tell you to go home, Alexandra, but you wouldn't listen.' He paused. 'How did she react when she saw you?'

'She didn't see me. I was in the dining-room, and she walked straight past.' Sandie's teeth had begun to chatter. 'I can't go back to the house yet. I can't!'

'You haven't much choice,' he said after a pause. 'Unless you come sailing with me. And you're hardly likely to want to do that,' he added, his mouth twisting sardonically.

In normal circumstances, Flynn's company was the last option she'd have chosen, but she'd have tackled Cape Horn single-handed rather than return to Killane at that moment.

She moistened her dry lips with the tip of her tongue. 'Please—I'd like to go with you. But I—I don't know anything about sailing.'

'Then I'll teach you. It's a grand day for a lesson.' There was amusement in his voice and something not so easily fathomed. 'Imagine how impressed your friends in England will be when you return to them, not just a star pianist, but an expert sailor as well.'

Sandie bit her lip. 'You—you know that isn't going to happen.'

'Well, you never know what the fates have in store.' Flynn dumped a couple of heavy canvas bags down into the boat. 'So, come aboard.'

She took a step forward, then hesitated, suddenly nervous. Couldn't she be leaping out of the frying pan straight into the fire?

'Having second thoughts?' Flynn taunted. 'Scared to be alone with me?' He laughed. 'Well, have no fear, Alexandra. A boat's no place for a seduction. When you're sailing, there's too much else to do. Besides, O'Flaherty's coming with me this afternoon, so he can chaperone you.'

'I'm not scared,' she denied, lifting her chin. 'Do I need any special gear? An extra sweater, perhaps.'

Flynn gestured towards some boxes and bundles already aboard. 'I can lend you anything you need.'

He turned to O'Flaherty, who was coming down the path from the house, with his arms full of other packages. 'We have a passenger.'

O'Flaherty's expression was forbidding. 'Is that a fact?' He fixed Flynn with a basilisk stare. 'Do you know what you're doing, or are you mad entirely? Haven't you set the whole house in an uproar already with your antics?'

'Yes, I know what I'm doing,' Flynn returned calmly. 'Now, let's get under way.'

To Sandie's relief, she was not called on to do anything to help, as *Graunuaille* set sail. The two men worked swiftly and competently round her as she sat, trying to be unobtrusive, in the stern.

It was startling to find how fast they were moving, she thought, trying not to feel uneasy as the landing stage, and the boathouse, and even Killane beyond them, became smaller and smaller. Nor had she realised quite how large the lake was.

Her only previous experience of sailing had been cross-Channel ferries, and these were no preparation for *Graunuaille*. Suddenly the boat seemed very small and fragile, and herself with it. She glanced up at the taut blue sails, and listened to the slap of the water against the planking, and realised she had never been as aware of the elements, or as close to them either.

The wind lifted her hair, making it stream behind her, and she shivered.

'Here,' Flynn produced a navy Guernsey from a bag at his feet and tossed it to her, 'put this on, if you're cold. And you'll find a life-jacket in that locker.'

She gave him an alarmed look. 'Will I need it?'

'I hope not,' he said. 'Unless I make you walk the plank.'

He was smiling, because it was a joke, of course, and she tried to summon up a dutiful grin in return, but it wasn't a success. And how could he make jokes anyway, when he must know how miserable she was—how shattered.

I shouldn't have come, she thought restlessly. I should have found a hiding place, and wept it all out of me. I can't cry in front of Flynn. He'd only sneer.

He'd have made a good pirate, she thought, stealing a look under her lashes—and what was she doing so far from dry land and safety with a man she didn't even trust?

What indeed? Sandie asked herself uneasily, and shivered again.

CHAPTER SIX

'YOU'RE very quiet. I hope you're not going to be sick.'

Sandie started out of her uncomfortable reverie. Flynn was still smiling, but his eyes were cool and speculative as they rested on her.

'I don't think so,' she returned, steadying her voice. 'She—she's a lovely boat. Have you had her long?'

'Not this one. She was built for me specially a couple of years back. But there's always been a *Graunuaille* at Killane. The first one I got my hands on had belonged to my father, and it was in such a bad state that it's a wonder I wasn't drowned.'

'The devil looks after his own, right enough,' O'Flaherty put in sourly from the tiller.

'It's an unusual name.' Sandie took a deep breath, trying to put her personal wretchedness out of her mind for a while. 'Has it any particular meaning?'

'Only an Englishwoman would need to ask,' O'Flaherty muttered. 'Don't they teach you any history over there?'

'Not a great deal,' Sandie admitted. 'And even less about Ireland.'

'And why should they?' asked Flynn. 'The fact is, Miss Beaumont, *Graunuaille* is one of the names for Grace O'Malley, who was a great sea captain and pirate in these parts when your Tudors were on the English throne.'

'A woman?' Sandie was intrigued in spite of herself.

101

'Very much so. She married more than once, and gave birth to a brood of children in between terrorising the seaways hereabouts. If you go to Cleggan one day, you can take the mail boat to Inishbofin which she used as her stronghold.'

He knew as well as she did that she would not be here to do any such thing, Sandie thought resentfully.

She drew a breath. 'She sounds—formidable.'

'She was that, and more,' Flynn agreed drily. 'She met Elizabeth Tudor face to face in London, and stood up to her too. But your Queen Bess was a bit of a pirate herself, so would make allowances.'

Sandie found herself smiling. 'I suppose so.'

'Do you want to follow in their tradition, and take a turn steering?'

Sandie sent an apprehensive look towards O'Flaherty, who glowered back at her.

'I think I'll just watch, if you don't mind.' She lowered her voice. 'Does O'Flaherty think all women on boats are unlucky, or is it just me?'

'A little of both, probably,' said Flynn calmly. 'Don't worry your head about him.'

On each side of the lake the hills were rising steeply almost out of the water itself, and to the west, the sun was already dipping behind the tallest of them, Sandie observed. It's getting late, she thought.

Aloud she said, 'Are we going much further?'

'Just to the island.' Flynn pointed at the dark mound crowned with trees ahead of them. 'I have some things I want to leave at the cottage.'

'Oh.' Sandie was taken aback. 'Am I actually going to see your private island? I thought it was sacrosanct.'

'It generally is,' he said after a pause. 'But I warn you, there's not much to see. You could jump over the whole place, with a following wind.' He sounded dismissive, almost terse. Perhaps he'd decided that O'Flaherty was right, she thought, and was regretting bringing her.

O'Flaherty muttered something under his breath that might have been swearing.

Sandie sent him a cool look. 'I'm sorry,' she said sweetly, 'I didn't quite catch that.'

'He said *Oilean an chroi*,' Flynn told her. 'It's what the place is known as locally. It means Island of the Heart.'

'Oh.' She digested this. 'That's—beautiful.'

'I'm glad you approve,' he said pleasantly.

As they got close, the sails came down, and Flynn used the engine to manoeuvre them into a small rocky cove, and beside the jetty which jutted out from the sloping rocky beach. Sandie could see no sign of any house through the clustering trees. She found herself wondering how he stood the isolation.

Once *Graunuaille* was safely tied up, they began to unload the supplies.

'Coming ashore?' Flynn asked casually as he heaved the last box on to the jetty.

She resisted the impulse to look at her watch. 'If you're sure it's all right,' she said rather stiltedly. 'If it's not an intrusion.'

'No, you're invited.' He handed her a couple of bulging carrier bags. 'This way I can make use of you. Just follow the track through the trees.'

Sandie had to bite back a cry of delight when she saw the cottage, standing alone in the middle of its clearing. It was a low, whitewashed building, with small-paned windows, and its thatched roof seemed almost to sweep the ground.

Flynn pushed open the door, and she stepped in, ducking her head slightly.

Inside, the air smelled musty and unused, and she stood looking round her as Flynn began to open windows. The door opened straight into the main living-room. It was spacious, with a large fireplace, and a supply of peats stacked neatly beside it. There was a curtained doorway, leading presumably to the sleeping quarters, while on the other side of the room, under the windows, was a modern sink unit, and next to it a cooker and refrigerator.

'I cook with bottled gas, but I also have my own generator for electricity,' Flynn explained, seeing her puzzled look. 'O'Flaherty's starting it up now. When it's running, and we've brought up the rest of the stuff from the boat, I'll make you some tea.'

Transporting the supplies took a couple of journeys, and by the time most of the things had been stowed away in the various cupboards and drawers, Sandie's arms were aching. She sat by the scrubbed table in the middle of the room and watched Flynn fill the kettle.

'It's a real home from home,' she said, after a moment. 'How long do you usually stay here at a time?'

'That all depends.'

'And do you always come here by yourself?'

He laughed. 'Now there's a leading question!'

She flushed. 'I—I didn't mean... What I wanted to say was—don't you ever find it lonely?'

'There can be worse things than loneliness. When I come here, generally it's for peace and quiet, and if that means solitude, then it's all right with me.' Flynn began to rinse out a big brown teapot. 'But I won't be lonely this time—not with you to keep me company.' He gestured towards the remaining bag of provisions on the table. 'Are you hungry now, or can you wait until supper?'

Sandie stared at him, aware of a faint frisson of alarm. 'I don't want anything to eat,' she said slowly. 'In fact I'm not sure if there's really time for tea either. We should be getting back. I have to see Crispin— talk to him—make arrangements. And we—we'll be late for dinner.'

'There's no gong to be obeyed here.' Flynn leaned back against the sink, his arms folded across his chest. 'We can eat when we like.'

'But I don't like.' Sandie got to her feet, her mouth dry suddenly. 'I really must go back to Killane. People will be wondering where I—where we are.'

'Then O'Flaherty will enlighten them. So sit down and wait for your tea in peace.'

'I don't want to,' she said. 'I want to go back to Killane—this minute!'

'Then I hope you're a good swimmer.' His voice was almost casual. 'Because that's your only way of getting there—unless, of course, you walk on water.'

'But—the boat . . .' she stammered.

'The boat is half-way back to Killane by now, with O'Flaherty.' He gave her a brief hard smile. 'Which means, my lovely Alexandra, that you stay here—with me—for all the days and nights till he returns.'

With total incongruity, the kettle began to whistle.

As if in a dream, Sandie watched Flynn make the tea.

'There's only powdered milk,' he said. 'Or will you take it black?'

'Neither.' She moistened her lips with the tip of her tongue. 'I just want to go home, right away.'

'So you still regard Killane as home.' Flynn set a steaming mug of tea and the powdered milk in front of her. 'That's interesting in the circumstances,' he added with irony. 'But don't be tempted to try and entrench yourself here, will you, darling? Your stay on the island is purely temporary, I assure you.'

Sandie pounded a clenched fist on the table. 'I'm not staying here at all!' she shouted. 'I won't be kept here against my will, and you can't make me!'

'I seem to have made a pretty good fist of it so far,' Flynn returned coolly. 'Here you are, and here you're bound to remain, until the boat comes back.'

She was shaking with temper. 'And how long will that be?'

He shrugged. 'As long as it takes. Until things at Killane—settle.'

'My God!' A thought struck her. 'Did your mother put you up to this? Did she tell you to bring me here?' Her laugh contained a note of hysteria. 'She tried to use the excuse that I might have some stupid cold to keep me out of the way. But that wasn't enough. I have to be—marooned with you. She's obsessed!'

'I wouldn't deny that, particularly where germs are involved,' Flynn said drily. 'But Magda's whims and fancies don't apply here. Bringing you to the island was my own idea entirely. I did not consult her, or

anyone else. Nor was I aware that you had a cold.'
He subjected her to a minute scrutiny. 'Have you?'

'I neither know nor care.' Sandie bit her lip.
'Please—please tell me this is some kind of sick joke,
and take me back to Killane. I—I won't make any
trouble. I'll stay in my room, I promise. I won't put
as much as one toe outside without permission, if
that's what it takes, but...'

Flynn raised his eyebrows. 'Is that the way of it?'
he murmured. 'You were to be a prisoner on the
premises. Well, Bridie will be grateful anyway, not to
be running up and down to you with trays.'

'Oh, naturally,' Sandie said hotly. 'Let's consider
Bridie's legs to the exclusion of everything else. Are
you crazy? You've—hijacked me, but you aren't going
to get away with it. When Crispin hears what you've
done...'

'Don't you think Crispin has other things on his
mind right now?' Flynn demanded with sudden
harshness. 'In spite of his soft words to you the other
night, you're not the centre of his universe, Miss
Beaumont. Knowing him, he's breathing a sigh of
relief that, without you, he has one problem the less.'

'You really think that no one else will care?' Sandie
asked furiously. 'That they'll just accept the fact that
I'm here—with you?'

'I think they'll be glad to. You'd be a severe embarrassment at Killane over the next few days. And
before that imagination of yours dashes away with
you, Miss Beaumont, allow me to elaborate the terms
of your—incarceration. Yes, we're here together, but
that's through necessity, not design. I doubt that
you're self-sufficient enough to survive on your own,

or I'd be sorely tempted to leave you.' He nodded sardonically at her astounded expression. 'The fact is, darling, in spite of the misleading impression I may have given over the last twenty-four hours, I've as little wish for your company as you have for mine.'

There was a silence, then Sandie said haltingly, 'I—don't understand.'

'You never said a truer word. I've brought you away from Killane, because, as you admitted yourself, my girl, Francesca hasn't seen you yet and I don't intend that she shall, until she's had a chance to talk to Crispin and try and sort out what the future holds for them. You're nothing but an unnecessary complication. Does that make things plainer to you?' He pointed to the chair. 'Now, why don't you sit down and drink your tea while it's still fit?'

Numbly, she did as she was told. 'Why did no one tell me that Francesca was coming to Killane? Warn me what to expect? It—it was such a shock.'

'I expect delicacy forbade them to mention it,' he said sarcastically. 'Or perhaps Crispin had qualms about booting you out as he's done with his other ladies in the past. After all, you have an excuse for being there, even if it's a specious one.'

'I thought they were separated—that they never saw each other.'

'That's no one's concern but their own,' he said curtly. 'The fact is, Francesca phoned me from Croaig Mhor first thing this morning, and I drove over to see her. I was on my way back when I picked you up on the road like the original drowned rat. She wanted to know the lie of the land at Killane—whether it would be convenient for her to see Crispin and talk to him, or whether he was otherwise occupied,' he added grimly. 'She has no illusions about your man.'

'And what did you tell her?'

Flynn shrugged again. 'I told her that Crispin was suffering from the mother and father of all hangovers, and to delay her visit for twenty-four hours,' he said. 'And I decided, by fair means or foul, to relieve Crispin of the distraction of you, so he could concentrate on his lawful wife, and hear what she has to say.' He gave her a bleak smile. 'Fortunately, you made it easy for me.'

'Crispin—knew she was coming?' Sandie closed her eyes. 'Of course he did! That's what he meant about your meddling. That's why they were both so insistent about me having this cold, and staying out of the way.' She gave a small wild laugh. 'Were they actually planning to lock me in, do you suppose? They must be mad, both of them!'

'Mad—and supremely optimistic. Killane isn't so blessed with bathrooms that you and Francesca wouldn't have met on the landing one morning.'

'She's going to stay there?'

He gave her an impatient look. 'Why shouldn't she? She's legally married to him, for God's sake.'

'But they're getting a divorce—aren't they?'

'Who knows?' Flynn said shortly. 'I've set up the meeting, but it's their own business to settle what comes of it. And while negotiations are going on, you'll stay discreetly out of the way. Let Francesca think, if your name's mentioned, that you were my guest at Killane—and my woman.'

'That's a revolting idea!' Sandie drank some of the tea. It was the strongest brew she'd ever tasted, and she almost choked.

'Well, at least we agree on something.' The lean face was harshly uncompromising. 'And while you're here, you have the freedom of the island, which is more than you'd have had at Killane. You can walk, and swim, watch birds, and fish. With luck, we need hardly set eyes on each other.'

She said hoarsely, 'You're such a hypocrite. You've done this just to spite Crispin because he was beginning to care about me.'

'Don't be a fool,' he said. 'You know that Crispin's only interest in you is your startling resemblance to the wife who left him, so don't start making excuses for him. But I'm not interested in spiting him. If I had been, I'd have taken you that first night when I found you there, all dewy-eyed and half naked in the music room. No, it's Francesca's happiness I care about, although it seems to be tied up in a man not worthy of her.'

He drank the remains of his tea, and dumped the mug in the sink. 'Now I'll show you your share of the sleeping accommodation.' He gave her a derisive look. 'It may lack the comfort of Killane, but at least I won't be locking you in.'

And I can't lock you out, Sandie thought, her heart hammering against her ribs.

She watched sullenly while he pulled out a small folding bed, a pillow and rolled-up sleeping bag.

'You can sleep in here, in front of the fire. I suppose by the laws of hospitality I should offer you my own bed,' he tossed at her over his shoulder. 'But I'm damned if I will, although you're welcome to share it with me if the mood takes you.'

'So much for your earlier assurances,' she said savagely. 'Let me tell you, I'd rather sleep on the beach!'

Flynn finished unrolling the sleeping bag, then he walked over to her, taking her chin in a merciless grip as he looked down into her face.

'That was a suggestion,' he said quietly and coldly, 'not a requirement. You're safe from my violent lusts, Miss Beaumont. I said, remember, if the mood takes you, and I meant it. From now on, if you want me, pet, then it's you that'll do the asking.' He let her go, almost contemptuously. 'And now I'll prepare supper for us.'

'Do you think I could eat?' she whispered. 'In these circumstances?'

'I know you'll be bloody hungry if you don't,' he said, with a shrug. 'But, again, it's up to you.' He gave her a long look. 'You're here because you must be, Alexandra, but I'll force nothing else on you. Is that clear?'

There was a silence, then, 'Is it?' he prompted ominously.

Sandie bent her head. 'I—suppose so.'

'Good.' Flynn sent her a mirthless smile. 'Now that we understand each other, we'll get along just fine. And to celebrate our first evening of bliss together, we'll have steak, and a bottle of wine.' He made a sweeping gesture. 'In the meantime, make yourself at home, Alexandra.'

He walked across the room, and, tugging the curtain aside, disappeared into the inner room leaving her staring after him.

Sandie swallowed the last morsel of steak, and put down her knife and fork.

'I'm glad you found your appetite after all,' Flynn commented sardonically, as he began to collect the crockery together. 'A hunger strike would have been too much to contend with altogether.'

Sandie flushed. Even if such a thing had occurred to her, she doubted whether she could have carried it through, in all honesty. As she'd sat beside the newly kindled turf fire, watching Flynn make the preparations for the meal, she'd been pierced with hunger, her mouth watering ravenously as the aroma of the grilling steak reached her nostrils.

Every mouthful had been delicious, she thought wistfully, remembering the buttery potatoes bursting from their jackets, and the accompanying tomato salad.

'Thank you,' she said awkwardly. 'You—you're a very good cook.'

'I like food,' Flynn returned as he carried the dishes and crockery to the sink. 'And I spend too much of my life being confronted by the plastic variety.'

It was odd to think of him in planes and skyscraper office blocks, she realised, and said so.

'You seem so at home here,' she added rather shyly.

'I am,' he said. 'Or I would be if Magda didn't insist on turning Killane into some kind of three-ring circus. When I'm heart-sick of trouble-shooting for corporations who can't get their sums right, I dream sometimes of buying myself a place, which is mine and no one else's, and breeding horses.'

'Does it have to stay a dream?'

'Probably.' He began to run water into the sink. 'When I was much younger I had my future all mapped out—one long panorama of boats and horses—even a suitable marriage. But nothing ever turns out as you think it will. I was found to have this gift with figures, and shown the kind of success it could bring me. I'd have been crazy not to go after it.'

'Do you still think so?'

He smiled faintly. 'The older you get, the more doubts you have,' he said. 'But my chosen career has brought me most of the things people want from life. I've travelled the world, and I've made more money than I can ever hope to spend.' He shook his head. 'And if I was in London or Paris at this moment, I wouldn't be talking like this. It's when I come back to Killane that I start to ask myself questions, and particularly when I'm here, in the place where I keep what's left of my sanity.'

Sandie found herself listening with a kind of wonder. It was strange to hear Flynn talk like this, without mockery or the aggression which had marked so many of their previous encounters. He wasn't like the same person at all, she thought, then caught at herself. But he *was* the same—and worse. He'd treated her abominably from first to last, and she couldn't allow herself to be beguiled into forgetting that—or softening towards him in any way.

'Kidnapping me isn't a particularly sane thing to do,' she said crossly.

'But remarkably effective, just the same. Don't panic, Alexandra. You'll be delivered back in a few days, in one piece, with no ransom demanded. I'm sorry there's no piano for you to play, but you can't have everything.' He slanted a glance at her mutinous expression. 'And there's no way out until O'Flaherty comes back for us, so you may as well relax and make the best of things, as I intend to.'

The best of things, she thought miserably. Until darkness actually fell, she'd still entertained hopes that she'd be rescued. She'd even entertained a momentary fantasy that Crispin might come sailing out of the sunset to her aid, until common sense had reminded her how impossible that was. No, as Flynn had prophesied, he was simply glad to have her out of the way.

'I still don't know how you got away with this.' She glared at him. 'You couldn't have known I was going to come down to the boathouse just then.'

'No, that was a piece of luck for me,' he said calmly. 'I was about to come and find you—invite you out on to the water.'

'But there was no guarantee I'd have ageed to come. What if I'd refused?'

'I'd have persuaded you,' he said, and smiled at her. 'One way or the other.'

'You mean strong-arm tactics, I suppose,' Sandie said with contempt.

'If all else failed,' he agreed casually. 'But I knew it wouldn't come to that. You'd been disappointed in love, after all, and left to kick your heels all day. Even if Francesca had taken my advice, and stayed away until tomorrow, you were ripe for a little adventure.'

She said shakily, 'Well, I got that all right.' She paused. 'But you haven't considered all the snags. I'm sure you've brought plenty of food, but that isn't everything. We could be here for days, and I only have the clothes I'm wearing.'

'I've thought of that too.' Flynn pointed to one of the canvas bags. 'You'll find a selection of your own gear in there. And before you start accusing me of raping your wardrobe, let me tell you Jessica picked the stuff out, not myself.'

'Jessica did? You mean she was in on this too? Oh God, I don't believe it! And I suppose the twins helped bring it all down to the boat.'

He laughed. 'No, although I dare say they would have if I'd asked them.'

'I didn't realise they all hated me so much,' she said bitterly.

Flynn gave her a surprised look. 'They don't,' he said. 'And why should they?'

'Because they helped you, even O'Flaherty. They let you do this to me.'

'But it wasn't through dislike of you,' he said quite gently. 'It's just that they're fond of Francesca. She's his wife, after all, and you're the other woman in this little scenario. We may seem an eccentric crowd, God knows, but this is a conventional part of the world, and they're bound to be prejudiced.'

'But I'm not the other woman,' she said wearily. 'Crispin offered me a chance to develop my music, just when I'd lost all hope, that was all. He was going to coach me, and in return I was going to be your mother's temporary accompanist. It was a business arrangement. I—I didn't know he was married. He never mentioned it . . .'

'I'm sure he didn't,' Flynn said ironically. 'And of course you weren't the slightest bit flattered or excited by all this attention from the famous Crispin Sinclair. And if he'd had one eye, a hump, and a hare lip it wouldn't have made the least difference, either.' He paused. 'Not to mention that you're the image of his wife.'

'Of course I was flattered,' Sandie said in a low voice. 'I wouldn't have been human otherwise.' She swallowed. 'But I didn't have the least idea about Francesca. I wasn't aware that she existed—let alone that we were the image of each other.' She shook her head. 'Yes, I found Crispin attractive. Naturally I did. I didn't know it was a crime.'

'Nor is it.' His voice gentled a little. 'The truth is, Alexandra, you were in too deep before you ever got here. You arrived to a situation you'd no notion of, and you wouldn't listen to a soul who tried to warn you.'

'Well, I'm paying for it now,' she said. 'You'll be delighted to hear I wish I'd never set eyes on Killane— or any of the people in it. I feel such an utter fool. I don't know how I'm going to face any of them again.'

'Well, for the time being, you won't have to,' Flynn said briskly. 'And everyone's entitled to make a fool of themselves once in a lifetime. The trick's to avoid repeating the performance.'

'I suppose so.' She bit her lip. 'And now, if it's possible to have some privacy I'd like to go to bed. I've got a terrible headache.'

'There's aspirin and stuff in that drawer over there. Help yourself to whatever you need.' He paused. 'Shall I open the bed for you?'

'I can manage.'

'As you wish. I like to go for a walk before I turn in, so you'll have the place to yourself entirely for the next hour. I'll come in quietly so as not to disturb you.'

'Thank you,' she said icily. 'You're all consideration.'

'But I need not be,' he said. 'This is as great a hardship for me as it is for you, Alexandra, so don't forget that, and push me too far. The only way we'll get through the next few days unscathed is if we both make a genuine effort to get on with each other. Goodnight.'

Sandie watched his tall figure walk through the door and out into the darkness.

Reluctantly she fetched the canvas bag, and checked the contents. Jessica, it seemed, had thought of everything. She took her toilet bag and towel, and went through the bedroom to the bathroom which had been built on to it. It was small, but functional.

She washed hastily, and got into nightdress and dressing gown. Flynn had said an hour, but how could she trust any of his promises? On her way back to the living-room she paused, looking enviously at the low, wide bed, with its clean line, duvet and fat, comfortable pillows which he would be occupying.

And I have to make do on that folding thing, she thought wretchedly. The age of chivalry really is over!

Her headache was getting worse by the moment. In fact she felt aches and pains in every muscle and joint, and struggling with the bed didn't improve her general malaise.

She placed the aired sleeping bag on the mattress and climbed into it, zipping it up to her chin, then lay staring at the glow of the turf fire. She was alone here with Flynn, in the middle of nowhere, and she felt terrible.

Magda wished this cold on me, she thought miserably, and felt tears pricking at her eyelids.

The cottage was making small, settling noises, and outside in the stillness, a bird called forlornly.

Sandie had never felt so isolated—so afraid. She could almost be grateful that Flynn had not adhered to his plan of just abandoning her here on her own.

But where was he? She squinted at her watch, and saw to her amazement that only about fifteen minutes had passed since he'd left. If time was going to pass as slowly as this, then the next few days were going to prove an eternity.

The first scalding drops of water began to trickle down her face, and she scrubbed them away fiercely with her fists. Flynn was not going to come back and find her weeping like a baby.

She had to think positively. Everything would be different tomorrow, and Crispin would come to fetch her. Whatever his motivation for bringing her to Killane, and even if he didn't care for her in the way she'd naïvely hoped, he was still responsible for her— and he wouldn't just leave her there.

My headache will be better too tomorrow, she assured herself, and I won't feel so totally grotty.

She tensed in every muscle as she heard the scrape of the latch, and lay very still, with her back to the door, and her eyes so tightly shut they were almost painful.

He came in as quietly as he'd promised, but she was conscious of every careful movement he made. Desperately aware that instead of going straight to his room, he had come to her side, and was standing there in the dying firelight looking down at her.

He said very softly, 'Alexandra?'

Her teeth sank sharply into the softness of her lower lips. She forced herself to remain motionless, to deepen her breathing in imitation of sleep, until, after some endless time, she heard him go, and she was alone.

She relaxed with agonising slowness, feeling her heartbeat pounding against her ribs. Because for a moment—a few brief seconds—she'd been tempted to respond—to speak—to turn to him.

And that was dangerous. That was the last thing in the world she should do. And Flynn was the last man in the world . . .

She pressed her clenched fist against her trembling lips. Tomorrow, she thought. Please let help come tomorrow—before it's too late.

CHAPTER SEVEN

THE TURF FIRE was blazing, and Flynn was building it higher and higher. And she was trapped here in this bed, unable to escape from the intense heat.

Sandie moaned feebly, flailing around inside the imprisoning sleeping beg, which was pressing on every inch of her skin, hurting her. Oh God, she ached all over, everywhere, and her head was the worst.

From some immense distance she heard Flynn say curtly, 'What's the matter?' Then, 'Good God, girl, you're burning up!'

'I know.' Her voice emerged as a hoarse croak. 'It's the fire. Please put out the fire.'

'It's been out for hours. Easy now.' She felt herself lifted, sleeping bag and all, and carried. She wanted to protest, but it was so much simpler to turn her heated face into the cool bare skin of Flynn's shoulder and let him take her wherever they were going.

But when he put her down, it was like being deposited on a bed of nails, and she cried out.

'Be still,' he said. 'You're going to be all right.'

Although she was so hot, her teeth were chattering, and that was funny. She tried to tell him so, but he was holding a glass to her lips, ordering her to drink. The liquid was icy cold, and slightly bitter, and she winced away from it.

'It's soluble aspirin,' he said. 'Drink it. You'll feel better.'

She would never feel better. She was going to die, and he would have to bury her, here on his island.

'Gladly,' he said. 'Do you want a headstone, or will a simple cross be enough?'

She wanted an angel—a six-foot one with huge marble wings. There'd been one in a nearby cemetery when she'd been a child, and it had always terrified her, but now she thought it would be a comfort.

'Someone to watch over me,' she mumbled from her sore throat.

'You need that all right.' Flynn sounded rather grim. 'Now, try and get some sleep.'

She'd no idea what time it was, but she thought it was probably the middle of the night, or the early hours of the morning. She tried to tell him she was sorry for disturbing him, but the words were jumbled and indistinct, because suddenly it seemed as if she could sleep—as if it was impossible for her to keep her eyes open even a moment longer.

There were dreams in that sleep, heavy, confused dreams, where she sailed across endless water in a boat with a high, carved prow. There was a girl at the helm, and she was laughing at her. A tall girl, with a fierce proud beauty, wearing doublet and hose, her hair tucked into a seaman's cap, who she knew was Grace O'Malley. But when she looked again, the girl's face was hidden, and her long blonde hair streamed in the wind. And still she was laughing.

And then Sandie was at Killane, standing in the doorway of the music room, watching herself sitting at the piano, trying to play Crispin's *Elegy*, but every note was wrong, and Crispin was shouting at her, getting angrier and angrier.

'You're no good,' he was saying. 'You'll never be any good!'

She began to whimper, and suddenly he was kind again, wiping her forehead with a cool, damp cloth, and telling her that it would be all right—that everything would work out.

I hope so, she thought, I hope so, and sank gratefully into a deep and dreamless darkness.

Her eyes opened slowly and wearily. It seemed to be daylight, and she was in a strange room, lying in a big bed. For a few moments she felt completely disorientated, then memory came flooding back, and she sat up with a little gasp. She was on Flynn's island, she realised, and she'd been ill. And this was Flynn's room.

She didn't hurt any more, but she felt incredibly weak and lethargic, and her head seemed so light it might float away at any moment. She sank back again against the pillows, assimilating, as she did so, that she was wearing a man's shirt in lieu of a nightdress.

But she'd had a nightie, she thought, frowning. The Victorian one with the little flowers all over it. She wasn't so far gone that she couldn't remember that. Nor could she ignore the fact that the pillow next to her had clearly been used, and that the covers on that side of the bed were rumpled and thrown back.

As she was assimilating this with mounting uneasiness, the curtain over the doorway was flung back, and Flynn came in. He was dressed in jeans and a thin dark blue sweater, and he was carrying a tray.

'So you're back in the land of the living,' he remarked.

'Yes.' Sandie had to repress an instinct to drag the covers up to her chin.

'How do you feel?'

'Rather odd,' she said truthfully. She paused. 'I—I'm sorry to have put you to so much trouble.'

'No need for apologies. You were sick, and you needed help.' Flynn sounded very matter-of-fact. He put the tray down across her lap, indicating the bowl of steaming soup which it held. 'Try and eat that.'

'Did you make it?' she asked doubtfully.

He grinned. 'I won't lie to you. It's some of Bridie's, out of the freezer at Killane. Does that make it more acceptable?'

'I don't know. I don't think I'm very hungry.'

'Then you should be. You've gone over twenty-four hours with little more than water.' He paused. 'When you have a cold, Alexandra, you don't take many prisoners.'

'It wasn't a cold,' she said ruefully, picking up the spoon. 'Before I left England, there was a virus going round locally—some kind of summer 'flu. We—the family, that is—thought we'd missed it. Obviously I didn't.' She hesitated. 'I hope I haven't given it to—anyone at Killane.'

'To hell with them,' Flynn said cheerfully. 'I hope you haven't given it to me. I can't rely on you nursing me round the clock with the same devotion.'

She gave him a pallid smile, and drank some of the soup. It was meaty, and thick with vegetables, and it tasted wonderful, rather to her surprise. She finished every drop, and almost licked out the bowl.

'Is it evening?' she asked, squinting at the grey light coming in through the window.

Flynn shook his head. 'It's supposed to be mid-morning, but there's been rain and thick mist since dawn. It may lift this afternoon, but I doubt it.' He slanted a smile at her as he picked up the tray. 'You're in the best place, Alexandra.'

'Mm.' She wasn't so sure about that. She moistened her lips with the tip of her tongue. 'Is this your shirt, please, and if so, why am I wearing it?'

'You were running a fever,' he explained. 'When it broke, your nightdress was drenched, so I sponged you off, and changed you.'

'Oh.' Sandie didn't look at him. He made it all sound very reasonable and even prosaic, but that didn't stop her blushing all over. And there could be worse to come too. She strove to keep her voice steady. 'I have a lot to thank you for, don't I? Especially giving up your bed for me.'

'As it happens, I didn't,' he said calmly. 'Even ministering angels need some sleep, and there was room enough for us both. But you already knew that.'

'Yes.' She stared down at the pattern on the bed-cover as if it fascinated—mesmerised her.

'Don't look so stricken,' he advised, amused. 'You were ill. You needed someone near you, and there was no one but myself.'

She said in a stifled voice, 'I—suppose so.'

'But you're wondering all the same if I took advantage of the situation.' Flynn shook his head. 'Never in a million years, Alexandra. When I make love with a woman, I like her fully conscious, and totally co-operative. You failed on both counts.' He gave her a brief, cool smile. 'Now, I'd stay where you are for the rest of the day.' He pointed at the wardrobe.

'You'll find more clean shirts in there, if you feel like a bath later. And there are books on those shelves under the window that might interest you. But rest as much as possible. Get well.'

'Thank you.' She still couldn't look him in the face, but there was something else she needed to know. 'You said I'd slept the clock round. That means there's a day missing for me. Did—has there been any—message for me? From Killane, that is.'

'None at all.' There was a grim note in his voice. 'Stop hoping, Alexandra. Crispin has other preoccupations.'

'You're so sure everything's going to work out just as you think! You can't manipulate people—people's lives—as you can money. Crispin told me that his marriage was over.'

'Crispin would tell you the moon was green cheese if he thought it would get you into bed with him.' His voice was cold. 'Look how he talked you into coming here by promising to turn you into some kind of prodigy.'

'Crispin believes in me—believes that I have ability.' She had to cling to that last remaining hope.

'And I believe it will snow tomorrow,' retorted Flynn. 'It's not your prowess at the keyboard that attracts him, you little fool, but that long fair hair, and the delectable way your body fills your clothes.'

'Stop it!' Sandie was blushing again. 'I—I don't want to hear...'

'I'm well aware of that,' he said curtly. 'But there are a few things you ought to know, Alexandra. You're not the first prize pupil Crispin's had. Francesca trod that path before you. He filled her head with talk of concert platforms and recording contracts, and for a while she went along with this because she was in love with him. But Francesca's got her feet on the ground, and she soon realised that though Crispin might fancy his chances as some kind of Svengali, she could never play the Trilby role. She was an averagely talented pianist, and she would never be anything more, and she knew it. That's why they fell out.'

'I don't believe you. Crispin told me about her—how she tried to use him.' Her denial sounded weak, even to her own ears. 'Anyway, why should he bother—with either of us, for that matter?'

'You really want to know?' Flynn's eyes were fixed mercilessly on her face. 'It's because he needs something to do with his life, Alexandra—since he lost his bottle, and vowed he'd never play in public again.'

Her lips parted in sheer incredulity. 'That's a lousy thing to say!'

'Like a lot of lousy things, it happens also to be the truth. The story for public consumption is that he retired to concentrate on composing and other interests. But the fact is he wrote that bloody *Elegy* of his, knowing fine that he was the only one with the capability of playing it, and then chickened out. It was as if he'd suffered some kind of block. He won't talk about it, and he won't have therapy. Instead he takes ugly ducklings of pianists and tries to transform them into beautiful swans.'

'I don't believe you.' Sandie shook her head violently. 'I won't believe you!'

'That's your privilege,' he retorted. 'But I'm telling you that he failed totally with Francesca and ruined their marriage. When he saw you—young, malleable, and the image of her—he must have felt fate was offering him a second chance.'

'And what about what I felt?'

Flynn said very wearily, 'Do you really think he gives a damn for anyone or anything but himself?'

He was silent for a moment. 'Believe what you want, Alexandra. Dream of being the second Mrs Sinclair, if that's what you've set your heart on. There've been greater miracles, after all. But don't depend on your ardent admirer setting sail to rescue you, even if Francesca goes back to Croaig Mhor. He's no hand in a boat at all, and O'Flaherty takes his orders from me.'

'Oh, yes,' she said bitterly. 'You're the lord and master of Killane, of course, and no one's allowed to forget it.'

'You're learning,' he said, and left her alone.

She lay for a while staring into space. She felt weak and weepy, and only the threat that Flynn might come back to check on her stopped her from bawling her eyes out. But she wouldn't give way, she vowed silently. She wouldn't let him see how much his cynical appraisal of the situation had upset her.

He's a complete paradox, she thought. Kind, almost caring one minute, and a total rat the next.

She didn't want to believe him, but she couldn't deny there was a certain horrible rationality about his revelations. After all, she'd seen Francesca, and been shocked by the resemblance they shared. If Crispin could fool her over something like that, what other deceptions was he capable of?

She gave her pillow a fretful punch. But she could prove nothing until she got off this island—and, more importantly, away from Flynn.

It made her squirm to realise how completely and humiliatingly dependent she'd been on him for the past twenty-four hours. Nor could she escape the fact that she'd shared a bed with him, however unwittingly.

And there was another night ahead of them, at least, before her ordeal could be over, she thought broodingly.

She gave herself an impatient mental shake and pushed the covers back, swinging her legs gingerly to the floor. She still felt horribly shaky, but she wasn't ill any more, and there was nothing to prevent her from returning to the sleeping bag tonight.

But not yet, she thought, swaying slightly as she stood upright. She would enjoy the undoubted comfort of Flynn's bed while she could.

She visited the bathroom, then made her way over to the bookshelves, scanning them critically. They contained a motley collection, spanning a number of years. She spotted some well-loved children's classics, a couple of her own favourites among them, alongside John Updike and Saul Bellow. There was poetry, some history, including Cecil Woodham Smith's account of the Famine, *The Great Hunger*, as well as a selection of tough modern thrillers, and a number of collections of short stories by Irish writers whom she wasn't familiar with.

Sandie hesitated over several of these, but finally settled for *Some Experiences of an Irish R.M.* by Somerville and Ross.

She climbed back into bed, almost thankfully, her legs trembling under her, and, rather to her own surprise, was soon thoroughly absorbed in the adventures of Major Yeates and his eccentric household and neighbours, and was giggling over Philippa's first experience of fox-hunting when she glanced up, and saw Flynn leaning in the doorway watching her.

'Oh, hello,' she said defensively, wondering how long he'd been there.

'It's good to hear you laugh,' he said. 'You don't do it often enough.'

Sandie bit her lip. 'Perhaps I haven't had a great deal to laugh about.'

'Maybe not, at that,' he said. 'What I came to say is that it's lunch time, and can you manage an omelette?'

'I think I could,' she confessed in amazement.

'That's grand,' Flynn said laconically, and vanished again.

The omelette, when it came, contained tiny mushrooms, and was accompanied by a thick, fresh slice of soda bread. Flynn brought his own food in, and ate it in a chair by the window, but Sandie didn't allow this to inhibit her. She finished every scrap.

'You're still very pale. How are you feeling?' Flynn asked critically.

'Much better.' She tried to sound casual. 'You'll be able to have your bed back tonight.'

His grin was sardonic. 'Will I indeed? Well, that's the news I've been waiting to hear!'

Sandie lifted her chin. 'And I'd like to know when I can go back to Killane.'

'You're not a very grateful guest. You have every modern convenience, including room service, and you're still desperate to leave.' Flynn shook his head in mock sorrow.

'Please don't tease me. When is O'Flaherty coming back?'

'Your guess is as good as mine,' said Flynn, shrugging. 'So relax, and make the most of the peace here. You can't pretend you found it restful at Killane, even when ignorance was bliss.'

'I didn't go there for a rest cure. I went genuinely to work.' Sandie encountered an ironic look and flushed. 'Oh, what's the use? You're never going to believe me!'

'Then let's talk about something else. Tell me about yourself, Alexandra Beaumont.'

'What sort of thing do you want to know?'

'Let's start with your family. How many brothers and sisters have you?'

'None, I'm an only child.'

'Well, that explains the singleness of purpose,' he said. 'Are your parents musicians?'

Sandie shook her head. 'No, but my grandmother was.' She was half-way through the history of that other Alexandra when she realised with dismay the implications Flynn would draw from it, and stumbled to a halt.

'Go on,' he said.

'If you insist.' She drew a deep breath. 'She was a failure, Mr Killane, just as you think I'm going to be. Isn't that what you want to hear?'

He said coolly, 'I'd prefer you to stop calling me Mr Killane in that idiotic way. Considering we've slept together for one and a half nights, I think you could use my given name.'

She gasped in indignation. 'But we didn't... At least not in that way.'

'More's the pity,' he mocked her. 'Isn't that what you expect me to say? Or shall we agree to make no more assumptions about each other's reactions to any subject whatever?'

Sandie bit her lip.

'Well?' he prompted relentlessly.

'Yes,' she said with a little sigh. 'I—I'm sorry. But it's what my mother and father think. It's why they never wanted me to take up the piano.'

'They'd have done better to have chained you to the thing—sickened you of it.'

'But they wouldn't have,' she protested. 'Music is my life.'

Flynn's brows lifted. 'But you haven't lived that long,' he pointed out matter-of-factly. 'And people change, Alexandra. They may sigh for the moon, but when they find they can't have it, they settle for something more tangible here on earth instead.'

'As you did?' She looked at him uncertainly.

'To an extent,' he said. 'But don't let me give the wrong impression. I've enjoyed my life. And each bend in the road is an adventure.' He was silent for a moment. 'So, what's the alternative to the concert platform?'

'Teaching.' Sandie sighed again. 'They'd be willing for me to study for some kind of diploma.'

'Wouldn't that be a reasonable compromise?'

'But I didn't want to compromise,' she said in a stifled voice. 'I wanted to go for gold—the glittering prize, the star at the top of the tree. Teaching's such—such a comedown.'

'It doesn't have to be. Not if you do it well—communicate your own love of music to your pupils.' Flynn paused. 'The man who taught me literature illumined my life. I'll always be grateful to him.'

'Please don't write me off yet,' Sandie said with spirit. 'Before I make any decision, I'll have to talk to Crispin—discuss it with him.'

'Naturally,' said Flynn pleasantly, and got to his feet. 'I'll relieve you of that tray.'

As she handed it to him, she said, 'I'm sure I'll be well enough to get up for supper.'

'Don't rush your fences.' His tone was laconic. 'It's no real hardship to wait on you.'

She was the one who was finding difficulties in the situation, Sandie thought, troubled, as she watched his tall figure disappear into the living-room.

The rest of the day passed uneventfully. As she alternately read and dozed, she could hear Flynn moving about in the other room, but he rarely intruded on her, and she told herself she was grateful for his consideration.

As supper time approached, Sandie got up, had her bath, and put on her own clothes. Her hair looked dull, and her face still lacked colour, but she felt as if she belonged to herself again, she thought, draping Flynn's shirt across the end of the bed.

The meal was Irish stew, cooked with neck of lamb and vegetables in a cast-iron pot on top of the stove. It was so hot it made Sandie yelp in protest, but Flynn told her that a burnt mouth was part of its tradition.

After supper he produced an old pack of cards, and they played Knock-out Whist, and Beggar my Neighbour, and he taught her the rudiments of poker.

And they talked.

Flynn told her about his boyhood, making her laugh at stories about the various boarding schools he'd attended as he trailed in the wake of Magda's career. But although he made it sound amusing, it must have been a lonely life for a small boy, she realised, recalling how the twins had talked wistfully about having a permanent home at Killane.

In turn, she talked about her abortive career in a solicitors' office, making light of the dull routine of conveyancing and probate, concentrating instead on the receptionist's mistaken belief that she was going to be the second Marilyn Monroe, and the senior partner's predilection for race meetings over appointments with important clients.

And she spoke about her music, and how much it had meant—about the hours she'd spent in practice, forgoing the outings to cinemas and discos and the dates with boys which other girls of her age took for granted. She told him about the competition, and her parents' ultimatum, and how Crispin's offer had come as a kind of salvation.

She was almost shocked to realise how late it was getting, and to discover how much she'd been enjoying herself—and how much about herself she'd inadvertently given away to the sardonic young man on the other side of the table. She'd more or less admitted that she'd seized on Crispin's offer too hastily without considering any of its wider implications, she realised with dismay. She stifled a small groan, turning it into a yawn.

'Tired?' Flynn gathered the cards together and stood up. 'Do you want something to drink—tea, or some warm milk?'

Sandie shook her head, looking down at the table, bewildered by this sudden awareness of him, and the intimacy they'd been sharing.

'No, thanks,' she said in a subdued voice. 'I—I'll just go to bed.'

'In here?' he said. 'Or with me?'

Her heart leapt uncontrollably in a mixture of excitement and panic. He was standing on the other side of the table, watching her, his face expressionless. He was making no attempt to touch her, or even come near her. Telling her, without words, she realised, that the decision was hers, and hers alone.

But she wasn't ready, she thought, shaken. She lacked the sophistication needed for such a deliberate choice, as she'd discovered when she backed away from Crispin.

She tried to force a smile. 'I—don't need a nurse any more.'

Flynn said, quite gently, 'That isn't what I was offering, Alexandra, and you know it. But no matter. If you need anything at all in the night, you have only to call me.' He smiled at her. 'Even if it's only for a drink of water!'

The pressure, if she could call it that, was off, it seemed, and she drew a deep, grateful breath, aware that her heart was pounding unevenly against her ribcage.

At the doorway to the inner room, Flynn paused. 'Do you need to borrow another shirt? I rinsed out your nightdress, but it's not dry yet.'

The alternative, she supposed, was to sleep in the nude, which she'd never done. And now seemed totally the wrong time for such an innovation, she thought, feeling a betraying warmth steal into her face. Flynn's faintly quizzical expression as he waited for her answer seemed to convey that he was following her train of thought with fair precision, and her blush deepened.

'Thank you,' she said awkwardly.

He nodded, and pushed the curtain aside, vanishing into the bedroom. He was back within a minute with a clean shirt, which he held out to her. 'Here.'

She wanted to say something casual and amusing about her raids on his wardrobe, but she couldn't think of a thing. All she was conscious of was the quivering mass of emotional uncertainty within her.

She walked round the table and took the shirt. Her hand brushed his, as she did so, and her whole body tingled in response to the fleeting contact. She drew a small, harsh, incredulous breath as it occurred to her how little she wanted to spend the night alone. And how much she needed to be with this man.

She said, 'Flynn—I . . .' and he laid a swift finger on her parted lips, silencing her.

He said, 'Go to bed, Alexandra. Go to sleep.'

He turned away, and she managed to return the pleasant 'Goodnight' he wished her over his shoulder as he went into the inner room, and the curtain fell into place behind him, closing him off as surely as if it had been a brick wall.

She supposed she should open her bed and unroll the sleeping bag, but she was shaking too much inside for any practical purpose, and she sank back on to her chair, staring sightlessly in front of her.

He'd taken her rejection very calmly, she thought confusedly, and he'd allowed her to have no second thoughts, although he must have known what was going through her mind. So he couldn't have wanted her very fiercely, or he'd have insisted—dismissed her last lingering doubts and fears—taken her in his arms—kissed her in that way that made her feel as if she was dissolving inside.

Even thinking about it...

She made a determined effort not to think about it. What she had to concentrate on, she told herself, was the undoubted fact that Flynn Killane was a worldly and experienced man. And although he might have found it entertaining to seduce her, it wouldn't have mattered much to him. And it certainly wouldn't have changed his life in any fundamental way.

Whereas for me, nothing would ever be the same, she realised in dazed wonder. My whole world would be overturned.

In fact, Flynn would become my world. And that's not what he wants. It's not what either of us wants. And I—I dare not risk it.

I dare not fall in love with Flynn Killane.

She covered her face with her hands, and sat for a long time, without moving, hoping and praying that it was not already too late.

CHAPTER EIGHT

THE first thing that struck Sandie when she opened unwilling eyes the next morning was the silence.

She sat up, unzipping the sleeping bag and gazing round her. The weather, it seemed, had done one of its about-faces, and the sun was pouring in through the windows and spilling in golden pools across the flagged floor.

The curtain to the bedroom had been neatly looped back, and there was a mug on the draining board, but apart from that there was no sign of Flynn's presence.

Sandie scrambled out of the sleeping bag and stood up, pushing her hair back from her face with sudden unease. It had taken her a long time to get to sleep the previous night. She'd lain awake for what seemed like hours, rotating her problems in her mind, trying to come to terms with the jumble of confused emotion besetting her. But she'd reached no sensible conclusion by the time sleep deeply and heavily overtook her. And now a swift glance at her watch informed her that it was nearly noon.

Why had Flynn let her sleep so long? And why had she woken to find the cottage apparently deserted? She bit her lip hard, as fresh anxiety welled up inside her.

Even in the short time she'd been here, she'd become used to the sound of shared living—his movements, the way he whistled softly when he worked in the kitchen. To wake and find that he'd disappeared, and she was quite alone, was disconcerting to say the least.

She grabbed underwear, jeans and a T-shirt, and shot into the bathroom, where she was brought up short by the realisation that his towel was missing from the rail.

What had happened while she slept? she wondered. Surely O'Flaherty hadn't returned with the boat already? But what if he had, and Flynn had decided to leave her here in splendid isolation for a few days while he returned to the mainland?

Oh, no! she wailed inwardly. He couldn't—he wouldn't!

She washed and dressed in record time, and ran out into the sunshine, looking almost frantically around her. She called out to him, but apart from the excited chatter of startled birds, there was no reply.

Beyond the immediate vicinity of the cottage, the undergrowth grew wild and thick, and almost shoulder-high in places, but there were tracks through it, as she'd discovered that first evening. She tried to remember which was the one which led to the jetty, but they all looked alike, and she made two false starts before she arrived, breathless, at the cove. She stood shading her eyes, straining over the sunlit water for the distant glimpse of a sail, but there was nothing to be seen, and with a defeated shrug, she walked back the way she had come.

Or thought she did. She found a clearing, right enough, but there was no cottage sprawling in the sun, just a tumbled ruin of grey stones rearing above the grass and bracken.

It's like a nightmare, Sandie thought faintly, as she backed away, or one of those weird films where everything changes in the night, and the heroine thinks she's being driven mad.

She tried once again to retrace her steps, only to find in front of her, at the end of the narrow path through the crowding bracken, the shimmer of the lake. I'm going in exactly the opposite direction, she thought in dismay, as she checked.

But just as she was wondering what to do next and telling herself no one could possibly get lost on an island this tiny, she heard, somewhere to her right, the faint sound of a splash.

She walked forwards down the path, bending her head to avoid the overhanging branches of the bushes and small trees which seemed determined to block her passage, moving quietly in her soft-soled trainers, and found herself on the edge of the stony beach of another small cove.

She didn't see Flynn at first, not until he hauled himself out of the water on to the rocks some yards away, his brown hair plastered, sleek as a seal's to his scalp.

Sandie felt an overwhelming sense of relief. He hadn't gone. He hadn't deserted her after all, she thought, taking an impulsive step forward, her lips parting to call to him. Then she realised with heart-stopping suddenness that he was totally naked and halted abruptly, shrinking back into the sheltering trees, aware that she was blushing like a schoolgirl.

Flynn stood for a moment, lifting his face to the sun, then began to dry himself, vigorously towelling the length of his lithe muscular body, and shaking the excess water out of his hair.

Sandie felt as if she was rooted to the spot. She wanted to turn away, to restore the privacy she'd unwittingly disturbed, but she couldn't.

She'd never seen a man without any clothes on before, or at least never in the flesh. Her parents had always been reticent about such matters, and quite apart from her almost ludicrous lack of experience with the opposite sex, Sandie had never felt the slightest curiosity about how the other half was made. It was women who were supposed to be the beautiful, the desirable without their clothes, she told herself bewilderedly. But Flynn looked—wonderful, lean and hard and utterly, arrogantly male.

She understood suddenly why the island meant so much to him. Why someone who lived most of his life in penthouse offices and hotel rooms in one major capital after another needed his own domain, where he could be entirely himself, dispensing with the basic trappings of civilisation.

And all she could do was spy on him—goggle at him like some kind of awful Peeping Thomasina, she thought in self-disgust, as she turned silently, and crept away.

This time, the path she took returned her straight to the cottage. She flew inside, and put on the kettle, before attending to her sleeping bag and folding up the bed. When he came back, she wanted to make him think she'd been there all the time, tidying up. The last thing she wanted him to know was that she'd been chasing all over the island looking for him—or, indeed, that she'd found him, she thought, swallowing.

By the time he lifted the latch, she'd spruced up the living-room, and was pouring water on to coffee granules in two mugs.

'Hello,' she hailed him with spurious gaiety. 'I was beginning to get worried. I thought you'd marooned me here alone after all.'

'You were sleeping so soundly, it seemed a crime to disturb you.' Flynn tossed his wet towel on to the draining board and took the steaming mug she handed him.

'Have you been swimming?' she asked, guilessly.

'I have,' he said. 'The water was wonderful. Why didn't you come and join me instead of skulking in the bushes like that?'

Sandie wanted the floor to open up and swallow her, but it refused to oblige. She stared down at the unresponsive flags, hating them.

'I didn't know you'd seen me,' she said in a low, mortified voice.

'I didn't,' he said. 'But when you're used to being alone here, as I am, you soon learn to detect another presence. And you're no Indian scout, Alexandra. You sounded like a regiment of soldiers in full retreat through those trees.'

'I didn't mean to butt in.' She was blushing to the roots of her hair. 'I—I just didn't know where you'd gone, that's all. I'm sorry.'

'Don't apologise.' He smiled at her, his eyes flicking over her slim, jean-clad figure in deliberate reminiscence. 'We're only quits, after all.'

'Yes,' she agreed in a strangled tone, turning away, and fussing with a tea-towel, 'I—I suppose so.'

'Although I had by far the best of the bargain,' Flynn added with unholy amusement. 'You were very beautiful, Alexandra, and also very helpless. I had to call on depths of chivalry I never knew I possessed before I could let myself touch you.'

'Don't—please!'

'Why not? I controlled myself then, and I've controlled myself since, although it hasn't been easy, and maybe it's as well that you ran away just now.'

'You—mustn't talk like this . . .'

'What harm can words do? For that's all there'll be between us, my beautiful one, until you decide differently.' He paused. 'I won't take, Alexandra, so you must give.'

'And if I—don't?' Her voice shook. 'If I won't?'

'Then it's your decision,' he said calmly. 'And in years to come, when you've confounded us all and become a great piano virtuoso, you'll wake sometimes in the middle of the night, and ask yourself if there isn't more to life than music. If there isn't a harmony of the emotions and the senses that you've missed out on.' Without changing his inflection, he added, 'Now drink your coffee like a good girl, and I'll take you fishing.'

Sandie leaned back against the slender trunk of the tree and closed her eyes. She'd spent the past three hours being scolded, teased, wildly encouraged and mildly sworn at; her jeans were soaked; she'd laughed until she was weak, and now she was relaxing, boneless with contentment, while Flynn stowed away the gear.

If anyone had told her that standing around up to her thighs in cold water, trying to coax a fish on to the end of a line, could be such fun, she would never have believe them, she thought, a smile curving her lips.

Yet would she have enjoyed such an afternoon so much in any other company?

Her heart lurched. I mustn't think like that, she told herself. I mustn't...

'You're looking grim.' Flynn dumped the rods down, and dropped on to the grass beside her. 'No wonder the fish would come nowhere near you!'

'That's not true!' Sandie sat up indignantly. 'I caught one. And you threw it back.'

'It was too young to be away from its mother.' He pillowed his head on his folded arms, and stared up at the sky. 'Isn't it a glory of a day?'

'It's been like a dream.'

He turned his head and looked at her. 'The trouble with dreams is waking up from them. And the real world's never far away, even here.'

It sounded as if he was warning her. She shivered slightly, as if a cloud had passed across the sun.

Was it all going to end, then? Would tomorrow bring O'Flaherty and *Graunuaille*? Was that what she was being told?

She shrugged. 'Then I suppose we just have to make the most of the dream world while it's there.'

'I always do.' Flynn paused. 'Are you cold? Are your clothes still damp? I don't want you to take another chill.'

'I'm fine,' she said. And physically, she supposed, she was. The virus had vanished, leaving no aftereffects. Her appetite was back to normal—in fact she'd eaten more than her share of the thick slices of ham and tomatoes which Flynn had provided for lunch.

All the problems were in her head—and her heart. She wished, for the first time, that she was more like the others of her generation—more streetwise and worldly. More experienced. She wanted to be able to analyse her feelings, rationalise them.

One day, it seemed, she'd been falling in love with Crispin. Now she was in even deeper emotional turmoil over Flynn.

I don't know what's happening to me, she thought.

It was as if she was caught up in some game, to which she did not know the rules. All afternoon she'd carried that burning awareness of Flynn inside her, although their relationship couldn't have been more prosaic. Any physical contact between them had been brief and purposeful, and he'd seemed more inclined to yell at her than kiss her.

He was making it clear that he'd meant what he said, that any move would have to come from her. Only she didn't know what to do.

'Come on, lazybones.' Flynn was on his feet holding out a hand to her. 'Let's get back. I have a feast to prepare for us.'

'Fish and chips?' Sandie asked as he hauled her up, and laughed at his pained expression.

'No such thing. I wouldn't insult fish of this quality with a frying pan. This is going to be a special meal.'

And it was also going to be their last together. He didn't have to come right out and say it, because Sandie knew. Their time on the island was ending.

She tried a bright smile. 'I can hardly wait.' She paused. 'I might even wear a skirt in its honour—Jessica put one in.'

'Then we'll both dress up,' he said.

Sandie went ahead of him down the path. When they reached the fork, Sandie turned to the left, but Flynn stopped her.

'It's the other way,' he said. 'That path only leads to the tower.'

'Is that the ruin I saw this morning?'

'So you found it. And did you see the ghost?'

'Ghost?' She swung round, staring at him. 'What ghost?' She saw that he was grinning. 'Oh, you're winding me up!'

'I'm not. I've never seen it either, but it's a privilege reserved for those with O'Flaherty blood, I'm told. However, I live in hopes.'

'Whose ghost is it?'

'A woman—one of the Joyces who lived round here, centuries back. There was always a great feud between the Joyces and the O'Flahertys, so when she fell in love with one of the O'Flaherty chiefs and he with her, there wasn't much hope for them—particularly as his marriage had already been arranged for him. So when she found she was pregnant, he brought her here, and built a small tower for her to live in, where he could visit her without anyone being the wiser. He called her the "woman of his heart", and that's how the island got its name *Oilean an chroi*.'

'That can't have been much of a life for her,' Sandie commented. 'Why didn't he just marry her, and have done with it?'

'It wasn't as simple as that. Simply by associating with her, he'd been guilty of a kind of treason to his clan, and his overlord had a short way with traitors.'

'So did she just go on living here with her child?'

'Not for very long. The story says the midwife who delivered the baby betrayed them, and the next time a boat beached here, it wasn't the lover but his wife, and her kinsmen. They murdered the girl and her baby in fairly gruesome detail, and burned the tower. Legend even says the wife cut out her rival's heart and presented it to the husband, as something to re-member of "the woman of his heart".'

Sandie shuddered violently. 'That's awful! Don't you ever feel the place is haunted?'

'Never once. There are few places round here that haven't a story attached to them, some bloodier than others. There's probably not a word of truth in any of them.' He grinned at her. 'I think the mistress probably got fed up with waiting around, and hitched a lift back to her own people with a passing fisherman. But O'Flaherty wouldn't spend the night here, all the same.'

'It must have been terrible for her—watching out for a sail every day—hoping.'

'Just as you do yourself,' Flynn said drily.

But I don't want to see a sail, she thought. I want to stay here forever, with you. The words sounded so strongly in her head, she was almost afraid she'd spoken them aloud.

She made herself meet his cynical gaze. 'Do you blame me?' she challenged.

'Not at all,' he said. 'But keep your chin up. Your ordeal will be over soon.' He turned and led the way back to the cottage.

Sandie followed in silence. His last comment had ended any lingering doubts she might have had—and any hopes too. She swallowed, fighting the misery that rose like an iron ball and lodged in her chest. The sensible thing—the right course would be to forget Flynn, and everything that had happened at Killane. To go back to England at the earliest opportunity, explain to her parents that it hadn't worked out, and get on with her life as best she could.

Only Sandie didn't feel sensible, or rational.

I'll worry about tomorrow when it happens, she told herself, lifting her chin defiantly.

Because, first, I still have tonight.

She was moderately pleased with her appearance when she looked in the mirror a couple of hours later. She'd had a lingering bath, and shampooed her hair, brushing it until it shone with its old lustre. She wished she had something else to put on other than the skirt and top she'd worn for her date with Crispin, but it was still one of her favourite outfits. And, she'd found, Jessica had omitted to put in her cosmetics bag, although her skin was glowing healthily after her day in the sun, and didn't really need further enhancement.

She pulled the curtain aside and went rather shyly into the other room. Flynn had just finished lighting the fire, and stood up dusting off his hands.

He smiled at her lightly. 'You put me to shame, Alexandra. I'm afraid all I can manage is a clean shirt and a shave.'

It was impossible to tell from his tone whether he thought she looked beautiful. She hoped he did. She wanted him to think she was desirable.

'I'd offer you a drink,' he went on, 'but there's only whiskey.'

'That would be fine,' Sandie said airily.

Flynn's brows lifted slightly, but he made no comment. He fetched a glass and poured her a measure of Jamiesons.

'Would you like water with it?'

She wasn't sure what she should say. Was it usual to offer water, or was he suggesting the drink should be diluted because he thought she couldn't handle it?

'I'll drink it neat.'

He studied her for a moment, then said, 'As you wish.' He poured himself a drink, and lifted his glass. 'Your health now and ever, Alexandra.'

It was as if he was saying goodbye, she thought, with a sudden chill. She took a cautious sip of whiskey and nearly choked. When Flynn had gone into the bedroom to change, she poured some of the drink away, and added a judicious amount of water.

Flynn had cooked the fish in the oven, wrapped it in foil with herbs and butter. Sandie thought she had never tasted anything so delicious.

'There's some cream in the ice box,' Flynn remarked when the meal was over. 'Would you like me to make you a Gaelic coffee, now that you're a hardened whiskey drinker?'

'It sounds wonderful!'

'Oh, it is. It can also be lethal.'

She found the truth of that as she sipped through the thick layer of cream to the hot dark liquid beneath. She gasped. 'How much did you put in this?'

'Enough,' Flynn sent her a laconic smile.

They sat either side of the fire. Sandie had kicked off her sandals, and her bare toes curled into the thick sheepskin rug that lay in front of the hearth. She could feel the warmth of the coffee uncurling through her body, making her glow. She watched Flynn under her lashes. His face wore an odd expression, remote and even a little weary. And the silences between them were getting longer and longer.

This isn't how I planned it all, she thought, taking her courage in both hands.

She said, 'Flynn,' and when he glanced at her, went on in a little rush, 'Would you make love to me?'

He was quiet for a moment, then he said, 'Probably, if the time and the circumstances were ever right.'

Sandie bit her lip. 'I—I didn't mean that. I meant—will you—please?'

There was another long pause, then he shook his head. 'No, Alexandra.'

'But you said only today—you implied that all I had to do was ask...'

'Yes, I know.' His face and voice were grim. 'I had no right to say that at all.'

'Why not?'

He finished his coffee and put down the glass. 'Because wanting isn't enough any more,' he said at last. 'People can't just—take any more without fear of the consequences. And there's no future for us, Alexandra. You know that as well as I do. And last but not least, because your innocence is a rare commodity which you should treasure.'

She looked at him, stunned. 'You're rejecting me?'

'No. I'm telling you that you feel this way because we've been penned up together here alone—and because you've drunk whiskey you're not used to. And I'm trying to ensure that there'll be no regrets when we leave here.'

'But I wouldn't regret it. I . . .'

'You don't know what you want,' he interrupted brusquely. 'A few days ago, the sun shone out of Crispin for you. Tomorrow—next week—who knows? I've been there, Alexandra. I was in love once, and planning to marry. But people change. Relationships falter. It's an uncertain world, when all's said and done. Let's make sure that we can at least part friends.'

'Are we—going to part?'

'Of course we are,' he said gently. 'And you know it. We have our own lives—other commitments. *Oilean an chroi* is a place apart, but the real world and the people in it are waiting for us, just over the horizon.' He got up restlessly. 'I'm going out to get some air before I turn in. I'll try not to wake you.'

She watched him go, then slid off her chair on to her knees on the rug.

It had all gone horribly, disastrously wrong, and she was at a loss to know why. Flynn had mentioned other commitments. Was he trying to tell her that he had a lover in New York, perhaps, or Paris? Jealousy knifed through her, and she wrapped her arms across her body, suppressing a little groan.

Or was it, even more damningly, that he didn't really want her?

I can't believe that, she told herself. From that first night he'd kissed her there'd been a hunger in him which even her inexperience could recognise. And now that she shared it, he was trying to deny it, it seemed.

Or perhaps it was the very innocence he'd told her to treasure that was the drawback, she thought suddenly. Maybe he thought she was just using him as an experiment, and didn't realise how much she wanted and needed him.

Somehow she had to convince him that she meant what she said. That she wasn't a child to be protected, but a woman to be fulfilled.

And quite suddenly, she realised how to do this.

She got up and went round the room, putting out the lamps until only one remained. Then, kneeling once more on the rug in the firelight, she began to undress. When she was quite naked, she put her clothes on the chair, covering them with a cushion, and settled down to wait for Flynn's return.

It seemed a very long time before she heard the sound of the latch. She stayed where she was, watching the dying flames of the fire. She sensed his abrupt halt as he saw her, heard his swift intake of breath, and turned then to look at him, smiling a little, lifting the concealment of her long fair hair from her breasts and scooping it back over her shoulders in a gesture as old as Eve.

He might have been carved from stone.

Sandie said his name softly and coaxingly and then he moved, crossing the room in swift strides, dropping on his knees in turn in front of her.

'We mustn't do this,' he said huskily. 'My beautiful one, we must not.'

She put out a hand and stroked his cheek, and the line of his jaw, and with a faint groan he captured her fingers and brought them to his lips. Then, gently, he drew her towards him and kissed her mouth, his hands holding her bare shoulders as if she was a flower he might damage.

Their lips touched softly at first, moving, exploring, learning the first tentative responses. Sandie could sense the restraint in him, the determination to hold back until she was ready to follow wherever he led her. She leaned towards him, deepening the kiss of her own accord, and his arms closed round her with sudden passionate force. His lips parted hers in unequivocal demand, and she felt the warm, silken thrust of his tongue against her own.

At last he put her away from him. His breathing was ragged, and there was a heated flush along his cheekbones. His hands slid slowly down from her shoulders to cup and hold her breasts. For a moment, she was unsure, because no one had ever touched her like this before, then, as he began to caress her, she gasped with a delight that was near pain as his sure fingers stroked the rosy peaks into proud erection.

Flynn bent his head, adoring each small, scented mound with his lips and tongue. She clung to his shoulders, feeling almost faint with pleasure, wondering dazedly what more there would be, and how she could stand it.

He kissed her mouth again, long and lingeringly, with warm, sensual emphasis, and sharp need pierced her deep in her body. A small, startled moan rose in her throat. Flynn smiled into her wide violet eyes, then lifted and put her down so that she was lying full-length on the rug, every inch of her exposed and vulnerable to the warm torment of his hands.

Using his fingertips, he began to stroke her, to mould, to outline and explore each curve, each plane, each soft, hidden valley, and all the time he watched her; watched her eyes for every fleeting manifestation of pleasure or apprehension; watched the soft rose colour of arousal blooming in her face, the moist fullness of her parted lips and the excited tumescence of her breasts.

Sandie was aware of nothing but this web of sensuous enchantment he was weaving round her. She had stopped thinking. Each sensation that assailed her was more agonising, more delicious than the last. He was touching her—kissing her everywhere except—there, in her most secret place, and he was doing it deliberately, she thought feverishly as her body writhed in mute pleading under his diabolically expert hands. He knew—how could he not know?—how she yearned for—that.

She couldn't believe her own wantonness—her own violent hunger. She was astonished at the painful joy that transfixed her as his hands and mouth teased, tantalised, brought her to the edge of some undreamed-of oblivion, then sent her back unsatisfied. She felt his fingers trace the length of her spine, drawn nerve-wrenching spirals on her buttocks, then slide round to her smoothly pliant thighs.

Her whole body tensed in need and anticipation. A voice she barely recognised as hers pleaded hoarsely, 'Oh, yes—please, yes!'

And then, at long last, his fingers feathered delicately against her, caressing her moist warmth, seeking out the little peak of sensitivity and strumming it softly. Reason, reality slid away. She was nothing but sensation, building exquisitely to some unimagined height, then pulsating into a thousand—a million small ecstatic agonies. Sandie cried out, her head thrashing wildly from side to side, until finally her body shuddered into peace.

For a while Flynn cradled her, his arms tender, his voice breathing endearments, telling her that she was wonderful, calling her his sweet, passionate angel. When he moved away from her, she murmured a little languid protest.

'Wait,' he said. 'That was only the beginning.'

She recognised movement, heard the rustle of his clothing, and opened dazed eyes, saw that he was stripping. When he came back to her, he wrapped his arms round her and held her closely, breast to breast, thigh to thigh, letting her experience this new pleasure of his bare skin against hers, kissing her mouth and her eyes, and the soft vulnerable places of her throat.

She was aware of the strength of him, the hardness pressing against her, and for the first time she was uncertain, afraid that she would fail him, that the ultimate joining of their bodies was beyond her capability. Then, as he kissed her and his hands began to coax her once more along the same sensuous, feverish path, she forgot to be frightened, even when his body covered hers, and she knew the moment had come.

He entered her slowly, and with the utmost gentleness, and her body welcomed him, opening like a flower to the sun. For a while he held her to him, rocking her softly, then the rhythm of his movements changed, and intensified, carrying her inexorably with them, urging her to mirror the deep, driving thrusts of his body into hers, seeking once again that dark implosion of delight.

Flynn's body tensed, then shuddered wildly against hers, as a harsh cry was torn out of him, and at that moment, Sandie felt her own inner being convulse into spasm after spasm of pleasure.

Bodies slick with sweat, they slumped together, breathing raggedly, and lay like that for a long time.

Sandie had never felt so utterly, gloriously weary. She buried her face in his shoulder, her eyes closing helplessly.

'Ah, no, sweetheart.' There was tender amusement in his voice as his lips brushed her hair. 'Why sleep on the floor, when we have a bed?'

And lifting her, he carried her into the waiting shadows of the inner room.

CHAPTER NINE

SANDIE cupped some lather in her hand, blew on it gently, and sent a large bubble wavering and wobbling towards the ceiling.

I know just how it feels, she thought, smiling as she leaned back languidly in the scented water, splashing it gently on to her breasts.

She doubted whether anyone in the history of the world had ever had such a blissful initiation into the pleasures of lovemaking. She'd slept in Flynn's arms, and woken some time before dawn to kisses, and the delight of his seeking hands. If she'd thought she had satiated from the earlier experience, her eager body soon taught her differently. Passion, tenderness and laughter had been exquisitely commingled into one tumultuous, unforgettable whole.

She had changed utterly, she realised. And not just through the physical transition from girlhood to womanhood. It was deeper, more fundamental and far-reaching than that. She was no longer just Sandie Beaumont—someone's daughter, someone's secretary, someone's pupil. She had felt the pulse which controlled the universe. She'd been absorbed into some timeless, spaceless ecstasy.

And she belonged to Flynn now, with a completeness beyond her wildest dreams.

She'd left him sleeping, and crept away to the little bathroom to be alone for a while, to treasure privately all the wonders which had happened to her—which he had brought her.

I never knew I could be so happy, she marvelled, smiling at the sunlight which filled the room. This was the tomorrow she'd dreaded, but now she was filled with new hope. After the magic, the beauty Flynn had shared with her, there was no way they could be parted, she assured herself. They would stay forever, together, here on this Island of the Heart.

'I've made you some tea.' Flynn's laconic voice from the doorway broke across her happy reverie. She smiled at him rather shyly, but invitingly at the same time, hoping with suddenly pounding heart, that he'd come to her, scoop her up, wet and soapy though she was, and carry her back into the bedroom.

At the same time, she was aware that he'd pulled on a robe, and that he was only carrying one beaker, which hardly suggested togetherness.

'Don't be so greedy, she adjured herself silently.

'When you've drunk it, maybe you'd get dressed,' he went on. 'The boat's down at the jetty, and I told O'Flaherty we'd be ready to leave in an hour.'

Sandie's head lifted, and she stared at him, her attention totally arrested.

'*Graunuaille*'s here—so soon?'

'I told you the real world wasn't far away,' he said with faint impatience. 'And we have to go back to it.'

'Yes, but . . .' Sandie swallowed, 'I thought—last night . . .'

Flynn's face tautened. 'Last night was a mistake,' he said harshly, after a pause. 'I don't expect you to understand, Alexandra. I just hope you don't hate me too much.'

Hate? she thought incredulously. Hate? Didn't he know—couldn't he guess how she really felt?

'But I want to understand.' She held out a pleading hand. 'Talk to me, Flynn, please. Tell me what's wrong. Last night was so wonderful . . .'

'And it's over.' The finality in his voice chilled her. 'It should never have begun,' he added quietly.

'Did I do something wrong?' She knew she should despise herself for asking, but the words came tumbling out before she could prevent them. 'Did—did I disappoint you?'

'On the contrary,' he said politely, 'you were all any man could wish.'

I don't care about 'any man'! she wanted to scream at him. I only want to know what you thought—how you felt—and why you're talking like this—frightening me like this?

She tried to smile. 'You make it sound as if it was— just one of those things.'

Flynn shrugged. 'Well, wasn't it?' he asked expressionlessly, then put the tea down on the windowsill and walked out of the room.

Sandie sat very still, staring in front of her. Oh, God, she thought. Oh, God, please don't let this be happening to me. Let it be a bad dream.

She touched the rim of the bath experimentally, willing it to dissolve and disappear, but it was all too real. Shivering, she hauled herself out of the cooling water, and grabbed at a towel.

She had heard of 'the cold light of day', but this was like the onset of a new Ice Age. Her golden joyous hopes were fragmenting around her. Other words, other phrases were beginning to beat in her brain too—like 'one-night stand'.

She wrapped herself in the towel, sarong-style, and went to find her clothes. Flynn's robe was flung across the bed, and the cottage was deserted. After last night's intimacy, his absence seemed to underline her sense of rejection, of isolation, and the pain of it was like an open wound in her soul.

How could he change so completely—and so quickly—from the warm, passionate man who'd taught her in the space of a few short hours that Paradise could be hers? she asked herself in appalled bewilderment.

Suddenly all the old-fashioned and despised warnings about 'giving in too easily' and 'men losing respect for you' seemed to have a ring of horrid truth about them. Last night might have been a wonder to her—a revelation—but to Flynn she was just another girl—an easy conquest among many.

She swallowed painfully. I can't believe it, she thought. I don't want to believe it.

And that, of course, was the trouble. She'd been fooled by Crispin. But she'd been even more gullible over Flynn. She'd known his reputation, and yet she'd still fallen into his arms. And now that he'd had her, he didn't want her any more, and she would never heal from the hurt of it.

But what else did you expect? Sandie lashed herself mentally. You can't say you weren't warned. After all, she thought broodingly, Flynn had revealed himself as a predator from the start. The feeling of closeness between them that he'd engendered since they'd been on the island, the kindness, and the laughter were all part of his stock in trade. He'd made her trust him, knowing cynically that he would reap the benefit.

But it was more than that, Sandie thought, as new pain constricted her throat muscles and brought tears stinging at her eyelids. He'd also made her love him.

When she was dressed, she went and sat at the living-room table. Her tea was cold, and she threw it away and made fresh, forcing herself to sip the hot, reviving brew while she considered what to do. She couldn't plead. She had to salvage what remnants of pride she had left. But she deserved a fuller explanation than Flynn's bald statement that it was all over.

She heard the sound of approaching footsteps and braced herself mentally. But when Flynn entered, O'Flaherty was with him, and all hopes of a private conversation were thwarted.

O'Flaherty nodded to her. 'Himself tells me you've had one of them virus things,' he said, giving her one of his narrow, critical looks. 'You look pale as milk, right enough.'

It was the nearest to a kind remark that he'd ever made to her. No doubt he guessed what had happened on *Oilean an chroi* and felt sorry for her. Sandie lifted her chin. 'I feel perfectly fine, thank you,' she said crisply. 'I'd just like to get back to Killane as soon as possible.'

'Killane, is it?' O'Flaherty muttered derisively. 'No one but a lunatic would choose to go there, the place in uproar as it is.' He gave Flynn a severe look. 'Well for you, Killane, if you sold the entire house from under them, lock, stock and barrel.'

Flynn gave a tight smile, and began to collect the belongings together. He and O'Flaherty worked fast, shutting down the generator, closing up the cottage and transporting the remaining perishables and other items down to *Graunuaille*.

It was less than an hour before the sails were hoisted, and they were on their way, making the most of the light breeze. Sandie sat in the bow. Everything inside her yearned to turn and look back at *Oilean an chroi*, but that would be too great a betrayal of how she felt. Flynn had been polite, but aloof, obviously distancing himself, making it clear that she had nothing more to hope for from him. And her dignity demanded that she should echo his attitude, and not let him see the pain that was destroying her.

Why? she thought, staring resolutely and totally blindly in front of her. Oh, Flynn, why?

Like all homeward journeys, it seemed much briefer than the outward one. Almost before it seemed possible, Killane was taking shape before them, the rays of the sun making the windows of the music room glitter like gold. As *Graunuaille* moved slowly to her mooring, Sandie wondered if Crispin had been up there, watching their approach, and if Francesca was with him.

When the boat was secure, Sandie allowed herself to be helped up on to the landing stage, and picked up the bag containing her gear.

'I'll take that.' Flynn removed it from her grasp and set up off the path, his long stride forcing her almost to break into a trot to keep up with him.

O'Flaherty had mentioned uproar, but Killane seemed almost deserted, the front door standing open to admit the sunlight. Kelly was lying in a patch of it, and he thumped his short tail in welcome when he saw them. Flynn paused briefly to speak to the dog and pet him, then walked into the hall and up the stairs, still carrying Sandie's bag. It seemed she had little choice but to follow.

He went straight to her room and tossed the bag on to the bed, then turned to face Sandie, hands on hips.

'What are you going to do? You realise you can't stay here. Not now!'

She lifted her chin. 'What are you trying to say— that Crispin won't want your leavings?' She had the satisfaction of seeing him wince. 'Or perhaps that was the whole purpose of the exercise,' she want on.

'It didn't even occur to me,' he said icily. 'But I wasn't thinking too straight at the time, as I've tried to tell you. Otherwise I would never have let it happen.'

'Yes, you've made that more than clear.' Sandie managed to control her voice, keep the instinctive hurt out of it. 'Now perhaps you'd leave me in peace.'

'Just like that?' Flynn's brows lifted in open amazement. 'Are you sure you're going to be all right?'

Sandie dredged up a scornful laugh from the depths she hadn't known before that she possessed. 'I lost my virginity,' she shrugged. 'No big deal.'

'Don't talk like that!' snapped Flynn. 'You sound like a different girl entirely!'

She shrugged again. 'Well, I suppose I am in a way. For which I have you to thank,' she added with an irony that wasn't lost on him.

A dull flush mounted in his face. 'Alexandra——' he began, then stopped, his face darkening in exasperation as someone knocked on the bedroom door. 'Who in hell's name...'

It was Bridie. 'O'Flaherty said you were back.' She glanced from one to the other, plainly diagnosing the electric tension in the air. 'Pardon for intruding, Mr Flynn, but there's Croaig Mhor on the phone this minute asking for you.'

Flynn muttered something under his breath that sounded suspiciously like an obscenity, and glanced at his watch. 'I'll be right there,' he said, almost wearily. As Bridie disappeared, he turned back to Sandie. 'I haven't time to talk now, but we can't leave things as they are. I'll see you later—try to explain.' He walked over to her and stood for a long moment looking down into her face. Breathlessly, she thought, He's going to kiss me... and her entire being awoke in anticipation and joy. She saw his mouth tauten almost in anguish, then he lifted a hand and stroked the curve of her cheek.

He said, quietly, 'Till later,' and the words sounded like a promise.

The door closed behind him, and Sandie sank down on the edge of the bed. She knew she was being all kinds of a fool, but she felt as if she'd been granted a reprieve. She reached for her bag and began to unpack it, knowing that she was giving the task altogether more time than it warranted. But sooner or later, she was going to be obliged to go downstairs and face everyone, and she was dreading it.

Eventually, when she had no excuses left for staying in her room, she walked along the passage, and down the staircase. The twins were in the hall, and James let out a whoop when he saw her. 'You're back! Steffie said you and Flynn had eloped, but I knew that couldn't be right. Flynn can't be bothered with all that old romance stuff. I told Steff he was just keeping you out of the way until the fuss died down.'

'Has there been a lot of fuss?' Sandie asked weakly, despising herself.

'You're joking,' said Steffie, her eyes round as saucers. 'They've been at each other's throats from morning to night. Jessica's moved out entirely, and gone to stay with a friend in Clifden.'

'Well for her,' said James gloomily. 'We've had to stay here in the middle of it. Bridie said we should offer it up for the Souls in Purgatory, but I don't see what good Mother having hysterics and losing her voice would be to anyone's soul.'

'Not to mention Francesca and Crispin going at it hammer and tongs,' Steffie added with a certain relish. 'Bridie said the atmosphere at meals was enough to poison the food in your mouth.'

Sandie bit her lip. 'Is Francesca still here?' she asked, trying to sound nonchalant.

'No-o-o,' James said scornfully. 'She went back to Croaig Mhor yesterday to get a divorce. Everyone knows that.' A thought struck him. 'Did you know that you and she are the dead spit . . .'

'Yes,' Sandie forced herself to say neutrally, 'I know.' She hesitated. 'Where—is everyone?'

'Mother's laid down on her bed,' Steffie said disapprovingly. 'She wants Flynn to send for a throat specialist from Galway or Dublin. She's mad with Dr Grogan because he said there was nothing wrong with her voice that time and holding her temper wouldn't cure.'

In spite of her own inner turmoil, Sandie's lips twitched as she visualised Magda's silent outrage at the suggestion. She said, 'And—Crispin?'

'Oh, he's in the music room, giving the piano some stick,' Steffie told her, wrinkling her nose. 'He's playing the same tune over and over, and when we asked him to play something else, he said the "f" word that Father Donaghue says is a sin,' she added in a tone of conscious virtue.

Sandie forced down a giggle. 'Well, that was very wrong of Crispin. I—I'd better go and talk to him.'

'Are you going to marry him?' James' clear eyes fixed on her face.

Sandie gasped. 'No!' she exclaimed more forcefully than she intended. 'No, of course not!'

'We thought that you might, that's all,' said Steffie calmly. 'It would have made everything neat and tidy now that Flynn's going to marry Francesca.'

The hall, the twins, the house, all reality receded to some strange distance. Sandie forced her numb lips to move, and heard a voice she hardly recognised ask, 'Is—is that what he's going to do?'

'Naturally it is. They should have been married years ago, everyone knows that. But now she's divorcing Crispin, there'll be nothing to stop them. Flynn's driven over there now to fix it all up with her. They can't get married in church, though,' Steffie added, frowning a little.

'What a shame,' Sandie managed from her well of shock and wretchedness.

'Are you all right?' James asked curiously. 'You've gone dead white.'

Sandie shook her head. 'I'm still getting over 'flu,' she invented swiftly.

'Well, don't give it to Mother,' James threw over his shoulder as he and his sister headed for the garden, 'or there'll be hell to pay.'

Sandie's thoughts were in chaos as she stood staring after them. James' parting words seemed to echo in her brain. 'Hell to pay.'

That, it seemed, would be the price to be exacted for loving Flynn. The hell of knowing that he belonged to someone else. That was why he'd changed from lover to stranger, she told herself dazedly. Because O'Flaherty had brought him the news that Francesca was not to remain as Crispin's wife—that soon she would be free again.

She stood, her arms wrapped round her body, wretched, confused, and aware of a feeling of total betrayal. And yet that was hardly fair, she tried to tell herself. Flynn had warned her there could be no future in any relationship between them. He hadn't tried to deceive her.

Indeed, if she was honest, she'd more or less forced him to seduce her, she thought, wincing with the humiliation of it. What a pathetic fool she'd made of herself! First it was Crispin, but that didn't matter—had never mattered.

Why couldn't I see that from the beginning? she asked herself despairingly.

Not that Flynn would believe in such a fundamental change of heart on her part. He only thought, cynically, that she was ripe for a little adventure, if not with Crispin then with the next man along. The skill, the passionate expertise he'd brought to her initiation hadn't been a sign of caring or commitment, she realised, but merely the means to an end, his goal being their mutual pleasure. Flynn hadn't wanted a shy novice in his bed, but an eager and responsive partner. Her ecstatic readiness to surrender must have amused him.

I mustn't think like that, she told herself. I mustn't—or I shall go mad.

With an effort she made herself move, forced herself to walk along the passage to the music room. She opened the door to a torrent of music played *fortissimo*. As the twins had said, Crispin was angry, and he was expressing his rage through the *Elegy*. Even through her own misery, Sandie could recognise that this was a brilliant, virtuoso performance in spite of the underlying fury which was inspiring it.

She stood quietly by the door, her head bent, listening as the piano tore its way to a savage *crescendo*, then stopped with shocking abruptness.

'So,' said Crispin, 'the voyager returns. I hope you enjoyed your cruise.' His voice bit at her.

She said slowly, 'It wasn't exactly my idea.'

'No? But I understand you didn't protest too much at the time.' He gave a derisive laugh. 'Poor little Sandie, what a romantic you are! I hope you didn't expect too much from your—interlude with Flynn. He likes to love 'em and leave 'em, as I've pointed out to you before—with one notable exception, of course.'

'Crispin, I . . .'

'There's no need for excuses or explanations,' he cut across her stumbling words. 'It's a pity my dear wife didn't come here with her ultimatum a little earlier, then maybe we could all have been spared this distasteful mess. But Francesca's timing was never her strong point.'

'She was the reason you brought me here,' Sandie said quietly. 'I was never going to be that good a pianist, and you knew it, but I looked like her, and you thought you could turn me into her.'

Crispin gave a scornful laugh. 'Oh, don't over-dramatise the situation, sweetheart. I'm no Pygmalion. Maybe I just like pretty blondes. As for your playing...' he shrugged, 'that's another thing you and Francesca have in common. You're both lightweights, artistically. You lack the purpose, the commitment that could have transformed you. You let emotion get in the way. That's the trouble with most women—they confuse emotion with wedding rings—domesticity.'

Sandie winced at the contempt in his voice. 'That isn't what you told me originally. You said Francesca had tried to use you for her career.'

'Did I?' He shrugged again. 'Well, what does it matter, anyway? She's going to get what she wants, one way or another. It was always Flynn, and it always will be. They'll probably settle in Tipperary and breed horses and children. Commonplace minds, the pair of them.' He looked at her stricken face. 'I trust you didn't have hopes of my errant brother, sweetheart—and that you didn't let things go too far on that island of his.' He gave her an unpleasant smile. 'After all, the resemblance between you and Francesca is almost uncanny, and it hasn't been lost on Flynn either, as you must have realised. But you would only ever have been second best with him, so I hope you haven't been—foolish, and indulged any of his little fantasies about her. It would have been a terrible waste of time, especially when he had the real thing waiting for him all along.'

Every word was like a barb, sinking sharply into her vulnerable flesh. But she refused to allow him to see how hurt she was. She lifted her chin.

'The only really stupid thing I've done was to come here in the first place.' She paused. 'I'd like to go back to England by the first available plane.'

'Oh dear,' mocked Crispin. 'You really do need to cut and run, don't you, darling? Will tomorrow morning be soon enough?' he added, glancing at his watch. He saw her hesitate, and went on, 'You don't have to worry about facing Flynn again. He'll be spending the night at Croaig Mhor, having a blissful reconciliation with my wife. And he won't hurry back here tomorrow. You can be gone long before he returns.'

Sandie bit her lip. 'Very well.'

'Then that's settled,' he said pleasantly, and turned back to the keyboard.

Against her will, she lingered for a moment, listening to the first plunging, difficult chords of the *Elegy* which he managed so effortlessly.

'Is there something else?' He paused, brows lifted questioningly.

'Just one thing,' she said. 'You're wasting your life, Crispin, writing music that only you can play. Your place is back on the concert platform—where you belong. Another viewpoint I share with Francesca,' she added gently, and walked out, closing the door on the crash of infuriated discords which greeted her parting words.

It was the only victory she felt she'd scored, and it seemed paltry in the face of all the other overwhelming defeats.

Her throat ached with tears she couldn't allow herself to shed, as she went up to her room. At the top of the stairs, she almost ran into Jessica.

'Oh, hello.' Sandie forced a smile. 'I thought you were in Clifden.'

'Even that isn't far enough away, with Crispin in a foul mood, and Mother behaving like Camille,' Jessica returned crisply. 'So I'm driving to Shannon to catch the evening plane.'

Sandie drew an uneven breath. 'Do you think there'd be a spare seat on it?'

Jessica shrugged. 'You could telephone and find out.' She paused. 'Can you not stand the atmosphere in the house, or have you become part of the general affliction?'

Sandie was silent for a moment. 'I—seem to be involved,' she admitted eventually.

Jessica sighed. 'I suppose it was inevitable, looking as you do. Crispin should be shot for bringing you here in the first place.' She gave Sandie a straight look. 'But is running away the answer?'

'It's the only one I can think of.' In spite of herself, Sandie's voice trembled.

Jessica sighed again, and patted her on the shoulder. 'Well, I won't argue with you. Now make that call, and pack your case. We don't have a whole lot of time.'

In a way, Sandie was glad of this, as she hastily gathered her things together. It prevented her from thinking. But not, she discovered, from hoping.

As she rammed her belongings into her case, she realised that she was on edge all the time, listening for the sound of a car, waiting and praying for Flynn's footstep on the stair—the sound of his voice. But she waited in vain, as she knew she must. Whether she went or stayed, Flynn would not be coming back to Killane. Crispin's cynical words had been right. Flynn was at Croaig Mhor with Francesca, planning his new life—the future that she could never share. The future that he didn't want her to share. He'd promised nothing, she reminded herself. He wasn't to blame for her foolish dreams.

She took one last look round the room to make sure she'd forgotten nothing, then carried her case to the door.

The rest of her brief time at Killane was taken up with goodbyes. Magda, muffled hoarsely in her scarf, was icily distant.

'It's probably for the best,' she said, as Sandie apologised for leaving her in the lurch. 'You were never particularly satisfactory.'

Only the twins seemed genuinely sorry about her departure, Sandie thought as she got into the car, where O'Flaherty waited in the driving seat with Jessica beside him.

He gave her a morose look. 'And about time,' he said. 'We'll have to drive like the devil to catch this plane.'

Yes, drive, Sandie thought with sudden violence. Take me away from here. Don't let me look back.

She could see her reflection in the car window, like a ghost. The girl, she thought, who was only the shadow of another girl. The girl who'd only been second best for the man she loved. The pain of that would stay with her for the rest of her life.

CHAPTER TEN

SANDIE'S fingers feathered the last few chords of *As Time Goes By*, then lifted from the keyboard, as she turned, smiling, to greet the scatter of applause.

The couple who'd requested the tune for their anniversary were clapping with the most enthusiasm, and Sandie lifted her glass of Perrier water towards them in a silent toast. Spending her evenings playing the piano in a busy wine bar, she was invariably inundated with offers of drinks, but she stuck firmly to mineral water all the same.

Her parents had been none too pleased about her new job, but she'd dealt with their protests gently but firmly, making it clear she had no intention of returning to secretarial work. She needed to earn money to pay Mrs Darnley's fees, and her own board and lodging while she prepared for her LRAM, she'd told them. Once she had obtained that, she would apply for a course as a student teacher, specialising in music.

It wasn't the life she'd envisaged, but it was a viable alternative, and she intended to make the best of it.

She sighed under her breath as she picked up the next request and studied it. Life had not been easy for her since her return from Ireland. Her mother in particular had demanded explanations for her sudden reappearance that Sandie did not feel capable of giving. She'd merely repeated over and over again,

173

with growing weariness, that 'things just hadn't worked out'.

Her mother, though clearly unsatisfied, had grudgingly accepted that this was the only excuse she was likely to get, although Sandie was still subjected to the occasional querulous questions, usually about Crispin. Mrs Beaumont had absorbed her daughter's pallor and abstracted air, and drawn her own obvious but incorrect conclusions. Sandie parried her enquiries and demands, thankful that her mother could not even guess at the truth.

She'd hoped that as the days which separated her from Killane turned into weeks, her memories might become easier to bear, but so far that hadn't happened. Flynn still filled her thoughts by day, and invaded her dreams at night.

As she began to pick out the first wistful notes of *Cavatina*, always a popular choice with the wine bar patrons, the words, *'He was beautiful'* sang sadly in her head. Everything, it seemed, conspired to remind her of *Oilean an chroi* and the brief idyll she'd enjoyed there. She'd never felt so close to anyone in her life—so right with him, and yet it had all been a giant piece of self-deception.

She reached the end of the piece, mechanically acknowledged the applause, and reached for her glass.

'Can you slip this one in next, Sandie?' It was one of the waiters. 'The guy over in the corner has asked for it specially.'

She took the slip of paper from him, and opened it. *Clair de Lune*, written in bold capitals, stared up at her.

For a long moment she sat frozen, looking at the words that danced in front of her eyes. She'd sworn she would never play it again. Certainly it wasn't the kind of thing customers usually asked for. It had to be some kind of horrible coincidence. Had to be.

She crumpled the slip of paper in her hand and swung round on the piano stool, her eyes searching the shadows of the dimly lit room.

The shock of seeing him, exactly where the waiter had indicated, almost drove the breath out of her body. Her eyes met his in anguished recognition, then she turned back to the piano, reaching for her bag with shaking hands.

'I'm taking my break now,' she told the waiter. 'Tell him—later, perhaps.'

She wanted to run, but she made herself walk at a normal pace to the swing doors which led to the kitchen regions, and the cubbyhole where she left her coat.

Mrs Westfield, who ran the wine bar with her husband, was just coming out of the kitchen.

'Hello, dear. Finished your stint already?'

Sandie shook her head. 'I'm afraid I have to go home. I—I've got a migraine.'

'Oh, that's an awful thing!' Her employer's instant sympathy made Sandie feel guiltier than ever about deceiving her. 'Would you like me to get George to drive you home?'

'Oh, no, it's quite all right. The fresh air will do me good.' Sandie was aware that she was babbling. 'I'll see you tomorrow.'

'Yes, of course. Now you take care of yourself. You're terribly white—like a little ghost.'

Sandie fastened her woollen jacket and dived up the steps to the rear entrance. She paused in the doorway for a moment, looking left and right, then put her head down and ran up the narrow lane which led to the main street.

'So there you are,' said Flynn, and his hand closed like a vice on her arm.

'Let go of me! Leave me alone!' She tried to shake him off, but all to no avail.

'Be still, you little wildcat! What kind of behaviour's this, when I've come all this way to see you?' There was laughter in his voice, and another element too, not so easy to gauge.

'Why did you come? Why couldn't you have stayed away?'

They stood facing each other under a street lamp. He was wearing a suit. It was the first time she'd seen him so formally dressed, Sandie thought numbly as she absorbed the elegance of its cut, the way the trousers hugged his lean hips and the waistcoat accentuated the slimness of his waist. His face was thinner, she realised, its expression faintly weary, and a little preoccupied.

'Because we couldn't leave things as they were that day at Killane. I told you that,' he said. 'There are still things that have to be said.'

'That's not necessary.'

'Well, I think it is,' he said curtly. 'For one thing, I need to know if you're pregnant.'

Sandie gasped, the colour storming into her face. 'Of course I'm not!'

'There's no bloody "of course" about it,' Flynn said with acerbity. 'Didn't it ever occur to you that it was a possibility, you crazy little idiot?'

She shook her head mutely.

'But you're sure that you're not?'

She nodded.

'Well, that's one problem the less,' he said with faint grimness.

'I hope you haven't spent too many sleepless nights worrying about it,' she flashed, caught on the raw.

'On the contrary, I've begun to think I invented insomnia.' His tone was bitter. 'Why the hell did you go off like that, without a word?'

'I said goodbye to everyone,' she said defensively.

'Everyone but me.'

'You weren't around.'

'But you knew I'd be back—I told you so. Why didn't you wait? Or at least leave me some message?'

She said flatly, 'I didn't want to be a nuisance. It was over—you said so. There was nothing else to say.' She wanted to add, 'And you had other priorities', but was afraid of sounding like a jealous woman.

Although that's what I am, she acknowledged painfully.

'You didn't want to be a nuisance?' Flynn echoed, with a small harsh laugh. 'God, girl, you were a thorn in my flesh from the moment I set eyes on you!'

'Then why did you come after me? And how did you find me, anyway? Did Crispin tell you where I was?'

'Crispin was in a profound sulk when I saw him last. I doubt if he'd tell me what day of the week it was. Not that I'd trust his answer if he did. And

Magda professed not to know where you lived, so I hired a private detective to find you.'

'Just so that you could put the record straight? Set your mind at rest about being a father? Provide me with an explanation I don't need?'

'Not just for that, no.' Flynn put out a hand and stroked her cheek.

Sandie jumped away as if she'd been bitten. 'Don't do that,' she said raggedly. 'Don't touch me!'

There was a silence. Flynn's eyes bored into her face for an endless moment, then he gave a swift sigh. 'So that's the way of it,' he said, half to himself. 'Well, Alexandra, may I at least drive you home?'

'You know where I live?'

'I was there earlier. Your mother told me about this job you were doing.'

Sandie groaned inwardly, imagining the effect Flynn's descent on them would have had on her parents. She wouldn't be able to avoid explanations this time, she thought dejectedly.

'I can walk,' she said.

'I know that, but I'd prefer to escort you just the same. My car's parked round the corner.'

There was a note in his voice which brooked no further argument. That and the firmness of his hand beneath her elbow. She let him lead her to the car in silence.

It was a far cry from the estate car she'd grown used to at Killane. This was long, low, and sleek, and it spoke of the power that only a lot of money can buy. This was the side of Flynn she'd never seen before. The wealthy consultant whose success meant he could command his own fees world-wide.

He helped her into the passenger seat, showed her how the seat-belt fastened, then walked round to take his place beside her. The engine purred into life.

She said, 'But this isn't the way home. You should have turned right.'

'I have a home here too, Alexandra. A temporary one at the Crown Hotel. We're going there first.'

'No!' The monosyllable sounded almost violent.

'To talk,' he said wearily. 'In comfort and privacy, rather than in the street.'

'But we have nothing to talk about.'

'Say that once more,' Flynn said levelly, 'and as God is my witness, I'll stop this car and box your ears.'

Sandie relapsed into a fraught and fuming silence.

The Crown was the largest hotel in the area, and it had recently been extensively renovated and refurbished. Flynn, it appeared, had rented one of the suites on the top floor, and as he asked for his key, Sandie debated the idea of making a scene in front of the reception desk, and as quickly discarded it. She hadn't the slightest doubt that Flynn's retribution would be swift and unpleasant if she did any such thing.

They stood in the metal cage of the lift like strangers, not even glancing at each other. When it stopped, Flynn took her arm again, and led her along the thickly carpeted corridor to a door at the end. He opened it, and stood back so that she could precede him into the room beyond.

Sandie found herself in a small lamplit sitting-room, with various doors leading off it. As she looked around, assimilating her surroundings, one of the doors opened.

'I thought you were never coming,' said Francesca.

She came into the sitting-room, smiling and holding out her hand. 'So, Alexandra, we meet at last. I'm so glad!'

Stiffly, Sandie held out her own hand and allowed it to be encircled by Francesca's warm fingers. She couldn't believe what was happening to her—the sheer cruelty of it.

'God, you're freezing!' the other girl exclaimed. 'Flynn, be an angel and rustle up some coffee for us before the poor kid turns to stone.'

Sandie tried to say she didn't want any coffee, but the muscles in her throat didn't seem to be working properly, and anyway Flynn was already leaving on his errand. Leaving them alone together.

'You look banjaxed,' said Francesca. 'Sit down, and I'll switch on this fire.'

'I can't stay...' Sandie managed.

'Yes, you can.' Francesca's voice was kind but firm. 'You can't run away again. And he'd only go after you if you did.'

She deposited Sandie on one of the sofas flanking the fireplace, and sat opposite her.

'Flynn's right entirely about how alike we are,' she observed after a pause. 'It's absurd—uncanny even.' She shook her head. 'God, if I didn't love that man so much, I'd hate him!'

'Yes,' was all Sandie could say in a small, wooden voice.

'You're probably wondering why I'm here,' Francesca went on, giving her another swift look.

'It's none of my business.'

Francesca snorted. 'Now that's ridiculous. If I found my man sharing a hotel suite with a woman, I'd soon make it my business.'

'Flynn isn't—my man.'

There was a silence. Then, 'I see,' said Francesca. 'And is that your final word on the subject?'

Sandie's hands clenched together in her lap. 'What are you trying to do to me?' she asked huskily.

'I'm sticking my nose into what doesn't concern me. I'm trying to find out if my oldest and dearest friend has a chance of happiness at last, before I go off and try and put my own life back together.'

Sandie stared at her, trying to make sense of what she'd said.

She said slowly, 'Go off? but where?'

'To find Crispin. He's in London just now, but he's off to Vienna in a couple of days to see his old maestro. It could mean that my dearest wish is going to come true, and he's going to return to the concert platform, and I want him to know he has all my love and support—if he needs it.' Francesca's eyes glittered suddenly, and she bit her lip hard. 'He may not, of course, but that's a risk I'll have to take.'

Sandie could hardly breathe. 'Crispin,' she said. 'You're still in love with Crispin? But I thought you were getting a divorce.'

'Never in this world,' Francesca said crisply. 'What I want is a marriage—a real one with a home, and children. A settled base for Cris to return to between engagements. That's what I always wanted, only he didn't. That's what I went to Killane to offer him, on condition he started playing in public again. God, he was furious! I thought I'd blown the whole thing completely, but if he's going to see Gunther Straubman, there's hope again.'

She gave Sandie a straight look. 'You know, I suppose, that Cris had some kind of psychological crisis about his playing. It started around the time we were getting married, only I was too besotted to realise there was anything wrong. And Magda encouraged it, of course. God, that woman's been a disaster to her children, although Flynn and Jess seem to have weathered her best.' She shook her head.

'Before I knew what was happening Cris was having panic attacks, swearing he could never appear on a platform again. I was worried sick about him, so when he suggested building up a musical career for me, I went along with it for a while. I thought once he realised how useless I was, it would make him want to play again. But it all went wrong, and eventually the only thing I could do to save us both from disaster was leave.'

She gave a wry smile. 'Flynn was like a rock to me, but then he always is. I use him shamelessly too. I even dragged him away from Killane when he needed to be with you. But that's the last time, I swear it.'

'But you were in love with him once—weren't you?'

'Back at the dawn of time,' Francesca said calmly. 'Oh, everyone thought we'd make a match of it, and maybe we did too for a while, but luckily we realised in time we were more like brother and sister than Romeo and Juliet.'

'But Crispin said...'

'Crispin says any number of daft things, when he's trying to justify himself.' Francesca shrugged. 'After all, it's easier for him to blame me than face up to the flaws in himself. Finding you, pretending that he could start you on the road to stardom as he'd failed to do with me, must have seemed like another reprieve from reality. As I said just now, if I didn't love him, I'd hate him.'

She meant Crispin, Sandie thought. Not Flynn. Aloud, she said, 'So you can forgive him for what he's done.'

'I don't pretend he's perfect, or that we won't have problems, but he's my man, and I'll go on loving him, and fighting for him, for as long as it takes.'

Francesca glanced at her watch. 'And now my taxi should be here to take me to the station. I'm catching the last train to London. I figure that if I turn up on Cris's doorstep like a waif and stray, the least he can do is take me in.'

Sandie stirred restively. 'Could I share the taxi for part of the way? I live not far from the station.'

'You could,' Francesca said levelly, 'but I recommend you stay here and listen to what Flynn has to say. Because no matter how many times you run away, he's going to come after you.'

'But there's really nothing else to be said,' Sandie began desperately, and paused as the suite door opened and Flynn came in accompanied by a member of the hotel staff carrying a tray of coffee.

In the flurry of activity which surrounded the coffee's arrival and Francesca's departure, it would have been easy for Sandie to slip away, but somehow, ten minutes later, she found herself in the suite alone with Flynn, sitting awkwardly on the edge of a sofa, drinking the coffee he'd passed to her.

Silence surrounded them, and Flynn seemed in no hurry to break it, Sandie thought, stealing a look at him under her lashes.

'Do you think Francesca and Crispin will make a go of it?' she ventured at last, putting down her cup.

'God knows.' His voice was curt. 'She's worth ten of him, I'll tell you that.'

'Perhaps she should have married you after all.'

'Heaven forbid!' He smiled faintly. 'Did she tell you about the one and only time we went to bed together?'

'No.' Pain pierced her.

'Well, it was a disaster. We knew each other so well that we were embarrassed to death. I couldn't even touch her, nor she me. We spent half the night apologising, and the rest in gales of laughter.' He lifted his head and sent her a long direct look. 'I had no such scruples about you, Alexandra. So if the idea's been put in your head that I was simply using you as a substitute for Francesca, you can dismiss it now.'

Sandie flushed. 'But you did have scruples,' she protested in a low voice. 'You—you said there was no future for us.'

'No,' said Flynn. 'You said that, when you told me music was your life.' He looked at her bleakly, his face stark and very pale beneath his tan. 'I've spent my entire existence surrounded by people who thought like that, and let their personal relationships go hang because of their obsession. I've learned to stand it from my family, but I couldn't endure it from my wife.'

He came and knelt beside her, taking her hands in his. She realised that he was trembling slightly.

He said, 'I knew that if I took you, I'd never be able to let you go. And yet the only life I could offer you wasn't the one you wanted.' He gave a small bitter laugh. 'God, I wasn't even sure I was the man you wanted, or if you were just experimenting because I was available. So it seemed better—not to take. I thought—maybe—if I never had you, I'd hurt less when you walked away.'

'But it was you who walked away.' The pressure of his fingers on hers was making her feel breathless, dizzy.

'But I was coming back. I thought—to hell with being noble and letting her having her chance of a career. After what we'd shared that night, losing you was impossible—like suffering some obscene amputation. I couldn't take that. So I decided to hang in there—try somehow to persuade you that marrying me would be the greatest thing for us both. That the music we made together—the kind of harmony we found when we were making love is the only kind that matters.'

He tried to smile. 'And if it turned out to be really Crispin you wanted all along—well, I'd be there to pick up the pieces.'

'You thought that?' Sandie said huskily. 'But it was never Crispin—not seriously. I think I had a crush on him, that's all. I—I didn't know much about men, or relationships. I'd been too wrapped up in my music to bother very much.'

'I know.' Flynn lifted her hands to his lips, kissing the soft palms very gently. 'Your innocence was the most perfect gift I'd ever received.'

'Truly?' Her heart was hammering. 'But Flynn, you could have anyone you wanted.'

'If that's the case,' Flynn said quietly, 'why am I kneeling here, feeling as if I'm under sentence of death—and praying to be pardoned, or put out of my misery? Because it's you I want, Alexandra, as my wife, now and forever, as long as we both shall live.'

She said simply, 'And I want you, more than anything else in the whole world,' and kissed him.

A long, slow, sweet time later, he said lazily, 'Are you sure you don't mind not being a concert pianist?'

Curled up on his lap, wrapped warmly and securely in his arms, Sandie smiled into his eyes. 'That was an ego trip I recovered from long ago, darling, and you know it.'

'But now you have this teaching career planned. Your mother was telling me about it. There might be some way you could go on with it.'

'I can always teach our children.'

'So we're going to have children, then?'

'You know we are. And horses too. All the things you dreamed about.'

'My only important dream has come true already.' Flynn's mouth caressed hers softly, and she surrendered to his kiss with a sigh, winding her arms round his neck.

When she could think again, and speak, she said, 'Flynn—will we live at Killane?'

'I don't think so, sweetheart. I love the place, but until Magda's prepared to relinquish her grip, I think we'd better find another home to start our married life in.'

Sandie stroked his cheek. 'Then—could we have the twins to live with us? They need somewhere too—and someone they can count on.'

'They've been in my mind as well.' He kissed her hair. 'We'll talk to them—see what they say. And now that I'm courting you officially, Alexandra, I'd better take you decorously home.'

She sat upright with a jerk, staring at him. 'You don't want me to stay with you? But you—we—haven't . . .'

'I know,' he said grimly. 'And I'm suffering the tortures of the damned at this moment through wanting you. But I love you, Alexandra, and you're going to be my wife, and I don't want even the least shadow over that—no guilt, no furtiveness, and no embarrassing your parents, who strike me as the old-fashioned kind. So I'm prepared to wait for you until our wedding night.'

'Do you think your self-control will last that long?' Sandie asked demurely. 'After all, a wedding takes months to arrange. The church is always booked ages ahead, and there are the caterers, and my dress . . .'

She broke off with a little squeal as Flynn's mouth came down hard on hers.

'We shall be married,' he told her when he raised his head, 'by special licence, my darling, as soon as it can be arranged. It's only a formality anyway. Our real marriage took place on *Oilean an chroi*—and you didn't bother with a dress on that occasion, or anything else either,' he added, his hand tracing a delicate and tantalising path from her breast to her thigh.

Sandie sighed unsteadily. 'First my career, and now my big white wedding! I can see my life with you is going to be one long series of sacrifices, Flynn Killane.'

'I'll try and make sure there's adequate compensation,' Flynn murmured, his teeth tugging sensuously at the lobe of her ear.

'But there's one sacrifice we'll both have to make.' Her voice was suddenly serious. 'Flynn, if we move away, we'll lose the island. We'll lose *Oilean an chroi*.'

'No,' he said. 'No, my darling. *Oilean an chroi* has served its purpose. From now on, wherever we are together, that's where our island will be.'

'In our hearts.' Her eyes shone at him with an abiding joy.

'You're right entirely,' said Flynn, and kissed her.

Harlequin Presents

Coming Next Month

Available in March wherever paperback books are sold, or through Harlequin Reader Service

In the U S.
901 Fuhrmann Blvd
P O. Box 1397
Buffalo, N Y 14240-1397

In Canada
P O Box 603
Fort Erie, Ontario
L2A 5X3

February brings you . . .

PENNY JORDAN

Award of Excellence

valentine's night

Sorrel didn't particularly want to meet her long-lost cousin Val from Australia. However, since the girl had come all this way just to make contact, it seemed a little churlish not to welcome her.

As there was no room at home, it was agreed that Sorrel and Val would share the Welsh farmhouse that was being renovated for Sorrel's brother and his wife. Conditions were a bit primitive, but that didn't matter.

At least, not until Sorrel found herself snowed in with the long-lost cousin, who turned out to be a handsome, six-foot male!

Also, look for the next Harlequin Presents Award of Excellence title in April:

Elusive as the Unicorn
by Carole Mortimer

HP1243-1

Harlequin
Superromance®

LET THE GOOD TIMES ROLL...

Add some Cajun spice to liven up your New Year's celebrations and join Superromance for a romantic tour of the rich Acadian marshlands and the legendary Louisiana bayous.

Starting in January 1990, we're launching CAJUN MELODIES, a three-book tribute to the fun-loving people who've enriched America by introducing us to crawfish étouffé and gumbo, zydeco music and the Saturday night party, the *fais-dodo*. And learn about loving, Cajun-style, as you meet the tall, dark, handsome men who win their ladies' hearts with a beautiful, haunting melody....

Book One: *Julianne's Song*, January 1990
Book Two: *Catherine's Song*, February 1990
Book Three: *Jessica's Song*, March 1990

HARLEQUIN
Temptation

The Pirate
JAYNE ANN KRENTZ

At the heart of every powerful romance story lies a legend. There are many romantic legends and countless modern variations on them, but they all have one thing in common: They are tales of brave, resourceful women who must gentle and tame the powerful, passionate men who are their true mates.

The enormous appeal of Jayne Ann Krentz lies in her ability to create modern-day versions of these classic romantic myths, and her LADIES AND LEGENDS trilogy showcases this talent. Believing that a storyteller who can bring legends to life deserves special attention, Harlequin has chosen the first book of the trilogy—THE PIRATE—to receive our Award of Excellence. Look for it now.

AE-PIR-1A